The

CleanUp

Woman 3:

Until Death Do Us Part

ALISHA YVONNE

Ebony Literary Grace

The CleanUp Woman 3:
Until Death Do Us Part

ALISHA YVONNE

Ebony Literary Grace
Memphis, TN 38116

ISBN 10: 0-9746367-9-7
ISBN 13: 978-0-9746367-9-5

Library of Congress Control Number: 2014920580

First Printing: December 2014

Printed in the United States of America

10 9 8 7 6 5 4 3 2 1

This is a work of fiction. Any references or similarities to actual events, real people, living, or dead, or to real locals are intended to give the novel a sense of reality. Any similarity in other names, characters, places, and incidents is entirely coincidental.

Prologue

Six months into Karma's psychiatric treatment...

The walk from my room to my psychiatrist's office was a long one. It seemed I couldn't get there quick enough. I had so much to say, and I knew he wouldn't be short of words either. I knew he eagerly awaited my visit just as much as I wanted to get there. I nearly tripped over my own feet a couple of times as I hurriedly walked to his office.

"Slow down, Jolley," Herman, the security officer stated. "No need to rush."

I turned my head over my shoulder to look at him briefly. I flashed him a brief smirk then turned around instead of responding. Nurse, Darla Mitchell also walked closely behind. Her eyes were buried in a thick file as we headed to Dr. Weisman's office. I always assumed the file was mine because she'd hand it over to the doc once we made it.

"File looking good, Nurse Mitchell?" I asked over my shoulder.

Seconds later, all I could hear was the rapid session of footsteps behind me, but that was all. I waited a few more seconds for a reply, but she didn't answer. I stopped walking and turned to her. Nurse Mitchell nearly bumped into me, stepping on my toes with her once-white, slip-on Nurse Mate shoes. She looked at me, seemingly startled.

"What's d'matter with you?" I said to her. "Didn't you hear me? I *asked* you a question."

She huffed just before lightly spinning me around by the shoulder and then urging me on with a small shove. "Keep walking, Jolley." She was calm, but stern.

I smiled inside, knowing I'd just aggravated the hell out of her. Nurse Mitchell was cool—better than some of the other nurses, but I liked doing things to make her think I was a little crazy, so she wouldn't try to get too close to me. I couldn't have her all up in my business with the doc and blowing all my plans. I'd spent enough time on lockdown as it was.

Six months in True Hope Psychiatric Hospital, also known as the nuthouse, had become like six years to me. A woman of my caliber had no business being housed like an animal. I not only had good sense, but I could clearly see that it was everyone else who had the mental problem. Hell, I didn't ask to be molested by my stepfather. I was a child, and he seduced me. And Cole—hmph! I only wanted to enhance his life. He wasn't happy with that first wife of his. That's the only reason I had her killed. Then, this dude went and married a new woman—Audrie. Now, if that didn't prove to everyone he was crazy, I don't know what will. Hell, he had *me!* I was not only damned near his personal slave, but I was also the best thing that could've happened to him after his wife's death. Audrie had nothing on me except her age. Who lets something like a slight age difference get in the way? Oh, yeah, that's right—Cole.

But for some reason, nobody seemed to notice I didn't belong in the nuthouse—nobody except Dr. Weisman, that is. Dr. Weisman, whom I so lovingly refer to as Doc, totally understood me from day one. I could see it in his eyes. He instantly won my heart, my mind, and my soul. The people, places and things I did before my sentence to True Hope were a distant memory once Dr. Weisman and I laid eyes on each other.

Just seeing the outside of his door excited me. Nurse Mitchell brushed her way to the door, and then stood in front of me, blocking my view of his nameplate. She was a tall, voluptuous, toffee-colored woman with nice-looking facial features and killer curves, but she didn't seem to know it. Plenty of women would give everything they got to have a shape like Nurse Mitchell's, but she never acted like she knew she had it going on. She seemed rather unhappy with life, but I refused to get to know her to understand if that was true. She placed the file by her side then knocked.

I straightened my blouse and twisted my knee-length pencil skirt so that the short split in the back was in the middle. All that was missing were a pair of stilettos, but the facility prohibited them, so I was restricted to a pair of black flats. It only took Doc a few seconds to respond to the knock.

"Come in," I heard his mellow, baritone voice say.

Nurse Mitchell opened the door then led me and Herman in. She walked over to Doc, who sat behind his desk, staring at the computer screen, and then handed him the file. He took the file without looking up at her then shooed her away.

"That'll be all for now, Nurse Mitchell." Doc never looked up from his computer screen. He kept typing.

I stood with my legs crossed and squeezed my thighs together as tight as I could before I oozed onto the floor. The sight of this smooth, caramel, hunk of a man with that bald head and salt-and-pepper goatee just did things to me—even when he wasn't paying me any attention.

Nurse Mitchell seemed to want Doc's attention as much as I did. "Do you want me to pull last week's notes for—"

"No, that'll be all," he said, cutting her off while still pecking on his keyboard. When he finally looked up, he addressed Herman. "And thanks, Herman. You can go to your post outside. I'll give you both a call once this session is over."

Herman nodded, but Doc didn't see it. He had quickly returned his attention to whatever he had going on that computer. Nurse Mitchell took it upon herself to give me orders before she left.

"Have a seat on the couch, Jolley. Dr. Weisman will be with you in a bit."

I walked over to the couch then sat, crossing my legs as best I could in my slender skirt. Nurse Mitchell shook her head.

"What?" I asked.

"Feet on the floor," she stated.

I uncrossed my legs then placed my hands flat on my lap. "Better?" I smirked.

"Behave, Jolley, or—"

"Um, Nurse Mitchell, thank you, but that will be *all* for now. You may leave," Doc said soberly.

That's telling her, boo! I thought to myself. Nurse Mitchell glanced at me. I smiled with my eyes—it was all I could do to keep from sticking my tongue out at her.

She sashayed out the door with Herman right behind her. He closed the door, and as soon as he did, I tried to give Doc his props.

"You told that bitch, Doc—"

"Shut up, Karma!" he snapped.

I was stunned. He'd never spoken to me that way. "But, Doc, you know Nurse Mitchell was chastising me for no reason."

Doc stood from his desk then walked over to his counseling chair and sat, staring at me, unblinkingly. I waited patiently for several minutes, hoping he'd cut the tension, but when he didn't. I spoke up.

"Okay, so what did I do now?" I asked.

"You tell me."

I shrugged. "If I knew I would. Don't I always speak my mind?"

Doc sat straight up in his chair. "Did I not ask you to refrain from the use of the Internet for social networking purposes?"

I nodded. "True. You did ask me that."

"Then, why am I still finding you on additional sites under the guise of RedKarma23?"

I laughed. At first it came out as a small giggle, but before I regained my composure, I had let out a hearty chuckle. Doc didn't seem to have a sense of humor at the moment. I cleared my throat then responded.

"Listen, Doc, you asked me to deactivate my Flirt Book and Chatter accounts. You said nothing about me blogging on Wroogler and Write Rest."

"Social media is social media. I shouldn't have had to spell them all out for you."

"Yes, you should have—"

"You listen to me, Karma," he snapped, cutting me off. "Now I've pulled a lot of strings to keep you comfortable here."

"Indeed, you have."

"And I can easily cut those strings if you don't adhere to the rules I've given you."

I sighed and rolled my eyes then rose and walked over to stand behind him. "Tell me, Doc: What are you afraid of?"

"Sit down, Karma."

I slid my hands over the top of his shoulders and began to massage him. His designer wrinkle-free, white dress shirt really did get in my way, so I slid my hands farther down so I could unbutton it.

"You're tense, Doc. Let me help you relax."

"Sit down, Karma," he repeated, this time with a firmer tone.

"Just let me help you." I managed to undo two buttons before he clicked on me.

He jumped up and turned to face me. "Sit down, damnit, and I mean now!"

"Okaaaaayyyy. Geeeeesssshh." I went to the sofa and sat down. "I don't know why you're overreacting."

Doc stood over me. "Here's the thing: Not everyone understands what I know about you."

"And what's that?"

"That although you are a little twisted in the brain, you have a lot of damn sense. You cannot be on those sites, risking a chance of someone figuring out that you don't belong in this institution, but rather in a prison. I could write up the paperwork and send you straight to do your jail time rather than prolonging it. But I'm keeping you here on a lie that says you still need treatment."

"Okay, Doc, let's keep it real. You keep me here because you get benefits by doing so. And as for me on those sites: You're just worried that I'm going to say some things that would be detrimental to your career. I've asked you to trust me. Why can't you do that?"

"Do you not understand that all the privileges I've given you—the extra time in the library, the relaxed dress code, the use of actual pens rather than crayons among so many other things I've given you—those are all things I have to justify in my reports. Karma, I'm risking too much as it is by being your doctor."

7

I rose from the couch and stared him right in the eyes. "Well, that's too bad because you *will* continue to see me, and you *will* continue to give me the perks I ask of you."

"Or what?" he asked sharply. I didn't know what to say. "You know, Karma, I *do* have a wife at home."

"Yeah, *and?* She means nothing to me."

"So, what are you saying?" he asked.

"I'm saying that although I started everything between us, it didn't take you long to comply. I can ruin you. I know you think it would come down to your word against mine, but the truth of the matter is if I cry rape, an investigation will have to be done, and I can promise you I'll win." I leaned in and pressed my lips firmly against his. When I pulled back, he just stared at me. "I love you, Doc. Let's not argue today. I didn't come here for this."

He backed two steps from me then began unbuckling his pants. "Go over and make sure the door is locked," he said in a much calmer voice.

A grin spread across my face so wide it hurt. "Now that's what I'm talking about."

I walked over to the door and locked it. Looking around, I could see Doc had already pre-closed all the blinds. By the time I walked back over to the couch, Doc was on his back, naked from waist down. I stood over him and lifted my skirt, exposing my panty-less bottom.

"Now, Doc, this is how I like to see you."

He pulled me on top of him, and then the real session began.

Lawrence

1

Six months later . . .

I decided it would be best if I just left work early. My desk phone rang off the hook, literally. I unplugged the handset, but the ringing wouldn't stop. Although I gave strict orders to the staff not to let Karma have phone privileges, she somehow managed to get to a phone anyway. She wouldn't stop calling—even when I threatened to have her on twenty-four hour lockdown—she wasn't fazed.

Karma had some issues, but she was more delusional than crazy. She had great sense. She was just one of those women who believed she should get what she wanted—when she wanted it. True, her stepfather's sexual abuse caused her to act dysfunctional at times, but Karma wasn't quite what I would diagnose as crazy. In my professional opinion, she needed to be locked up in the general prison population. She was fully aware of what she was doing each time she killed or caused harm to others. But there was something about that girl that could make a man want to live dangerously, and namely, that man was me.

I should've had better control of my loins when it came to Karma, but I didn't. She wasn't the first patient to come on to me, but she was the only one who tempted me. The nonstop ringing of my office line sent me packing for the day. It was 2:00 P.M., and I'd seen my scheduled patients, so off to have a drink I went. The receptionist stopped me in the lobby as I headed out.

"Dr. Weisman," Ms. Anderson called from behind her desk. She pressed a button on the multi-line system then set the phone receiver on its base. "There's a call, holding for you on Line 7, but I see you're on your way out. Should I take a message?"

I slowly approached her desk. "Would you happen to know who's on the line?" I asked in a low, cautious tone.

She leaned in and said, "No, but I can see that it's an outside line on the ID." Her voice was nearly a whisper, but her face showed confusion as to why we were talking low.

"Okay, no problem," I spoke up. "I'll take the call."

Ms. Anderson pressed a button then spoke into the phone. "Thank you for holding. Dr. Weisman will take your call now."

I answered as soon as she handed me the receiver. "This is Dr. Lawrence Weisman. How may I help you?"

"You bastard!" she yelled. "Why have you been ignoring my calls?"

"Excuse me?" I frowned.

"Oh, you are NOT excused! You heard me. I will *not* be ignored!"

I glanced at Ms. Anderson briefly. She shuffled a few sheets of paper on her desk then turned to type on her computer keyboard. I stretched the receiver cord as far as it would go, and then turned my back to finish the call.

"Um, ma'am, that would not be the case."

"Doc, this is Karma you're speaking to."

"Oh, yes, ma'am. I am well aware of who you are."

I glanced over my shoulder. Ms. Anderson continued her job. She didn't seem to be paying me any mind. Karma proceeded to let me have it.

"I'm not going to play these games with you, Doc. I asked to see you three days ago. Why haven't you requested my visit?"

"We have strict rules here, ma'am. I can only comply with the guidelines."

"Get me in there to see you tomorrow or else you will *not* like my wrath!" She sounded as if she spoke through clenched teeth.

"I'll see what I can do, ma'am."

"Make it happen!" She hung up.

I took a deep breath then turned to hand Ms. Anderson the receiver.

"Um, thank you for the call, Ms. Anderson."

She spun around in her chair and smiled. "Oh, are you done already?"

"Yes. I'm gone for the day, so if there are any more calls, please send them to my voice mail."

"Will do," she said, taking the receiver from me and placing it back on its base. "You have a great afternoon, and I'll see you back here tomorrow."

I nodded then turned to leave, unable to say more due to a million thoughts racing in my brain. I pulled out my cell and called my buddy who was also a colleague.

"Lawrence, how's it going?" he said as he answered his cell.

"Not good, Steve."

"Uh-oh. I'm almost afraid to ask."

"As you should be."

"Are you still working?"

"No. I'm on my way out as we speak—gotta have a drink. What time will you finish for the day?"

"I'm looking at another hour here," he said.

"Alright, listen. I'm heading over to Midtown for happy hour."

"Bar Louie?"

"Yeah. Look for me on the patio. I'll probably have downed a few by the time you make it, but I should still be good for another one once you get there."

"Bet. See you soon, buddy."

We might've hung up at the same time—I'm not sure. All I know is once I opened the door to my brand new BMW Z4, the hands-free Bluetooth kicked on. I pressed END CALL without thinking. My wife wasn't too happy when I got the two-seater because she still had hopes of having children someday.

I knew Aisha would be my wife from the first day I laid eyes on her. She'd just finished modeling at a local charity event. I'd never been drawn to light-skinned women—mocha was my preference—but Aisha was stunning. Her 5'10 frame and long, dark hair along with her

Japanese and African American features gave her a sex appeal that commanded attention. Apparently she couldn't say no to me either because it was fourteen years ago that we walked down the aisle and said I do's after only six months of dating. The greatest problem for us over the years dealt with her fertility issues, but that only bothered her—not me. She was the one in love with the thought of raising kids. It didn't bother me whether we ever had children. Unbeknownst to Aisha, we had one other problem that concerned me, and that was my patient by the name of Karma.

The fact that I'd been sleeping around with that girl for about a year was insanity itself. I needed to stretch out on somebody's couch and express my anxieties over the situation, but that would more than likely get me sent to jail. A psychiatrist should never cross the lines with his patients, and I was well aware of that. So, why couldn't I contain myself? That was the million-dollar question I could never answer. I had no answer.

A total of three Jack and Cokes were a thing of the past by the time Steve walked out onto the patio to meet me. I stood then slapped my hand into his just before greeting him with the one-armed hug. He took a seat then looked around and noticed we were the only two sitting on the patio.

"What happened? Did you wave everyone off before they could come over and join you, man?" he asked.

I shook my head. "No, it must've been the damn-it-I'll-bite-you look on my face that made them sit elsewhere."

He laughed, but I wasn't in the mood yet. He certainly noticed. "You're not laughing."

"My life is complicated, man."

"Oh, hell. It's Karma, isn't it?"

I nodded. "Who else? Do you know she figured a way to call the front desk to ask for me, making the call look like it was from an outside line?"

Steve shook his head. "Hey, let me order a drink before you say anything else. I know you're the one she's stressing, but just listening to the bullshit makes me tired."

Steve turned and waved a waitress over. It didn't seem to matter to him whether she was the one assigned to serve us. He ordered three different appetizers for us to munch on and two Jack and Cokes. I looked at the time on my phone and wondered if I needed to call the Missus to let her know I might be late coming home. Steve meant exactly what he said. He didn't bother asking the first question until he had taken at least two sips of his drink.

"Okay. So, let me get this straight before you try to explain anything. You still haven't ended things with this girl, have you?" he asked.

"How can I? She's still a patient of mine. I have to see her."

Steve sat up and leaned in to me. "Yeah, but you *don't* have to fuck her," he said in a low but harsh tone.

"She's blackmailing me."

"Imagine that! How does a mental patient blackmail her psychiatrist?"

"For sex," I snapped.

Steve giggled then sipped his drink. "Unbeliev-able." He shook his head, took another sip then said, "Un-fuckin-believable."

"What's unbelievable?"

"You are!" It was clear Steve was mad when he slammed his near empty glass down, rattling the ice. "I told your ass more than six months ago, when you first told me what you were doing, to put a stop to the shit. Now you want to give me some bull about she's blackmailing you."

"She is!"

"You love fucking that girl, Lawrence—that's why you haven't stopped, and you know it!" Steve's voice carried just above average that time.

"Hold it down, man. I-hear-you."

"You should've heard me six months ago!"

Our waitress came over to offer more drinks. I declined, but Steve ordered another one. As soon as the waitress walked away, he tore into me some more.

"Listen, I'm not losing my career for you," he said. "I'm sorry, but I will not stick my neck out for you on this one."

"Are you freaking kidding me, man? If you think for one second, Dr. Steven M. Johnson, that I would have you lie on my behalf and risk your career, you don't know me like I thought you did. Hell, I'm not trying to lose my own career, either."

"I can't tell," he snapped.

"What?"

"You heard me. I can't tell. The shit you're doing with Karma is straight up Roulette. For every day you don't get that girl out of the way, you take a chance on losing everything you've got—and that includes your career, your wife, your freedom, and your entire life as you know it." We stared at each other for a few seconds. "I'm telling you now, the day it comes down to my life or yours, I'm saving my own ass. I will tell the authorities what's necessary to keep them from throwing me to the dogs, too. In fact, stop telling me about you and this girl. The less I know the better."

I didn't talk anymore as Steve and I finished the appetizers and drinks. We mostly talked on our cells and texted people the remainder of the time we were there. I let my wife know I would be home late, so she wouldn't worry. I still needed to clear my mind. I knew Steve was right about getting Karma out of the way, but I had no idea how to do that. I needed a plan like yesterday.

Karma

2

Doc really should be ashamed of himself. Everybody knows a doctor-patient relationship should remain professional at all times. So, rolling around naked on the floor and couch of Dr. Weisman's office was without a doubt unethical, but I guess somebody should've told him that before I got a hold of him. All the book sense in the world wouldn't have made him smart enough not to fool with me. In fact, that made him *dumb*, but who's complaining? Certainly not me. The man was just plain handsome— about six-two with a lean frame, a smooth caramel complexion, strong jaw-line, bald head, and a neatly trimmed salt-and-pepper goatee. He was a little older than I was accustomed to, but a few years or so past forty didn't bother me none.

Doc had already told me a number of times I wasn't crazy and that I just played crazy. I wondered what that made him, knowing the things I was capable of—he was either missing a few screws in his brain, or he was simply in love with me. I'd say it was the latter.

He was not going to play me—I meant that. My stepfather played me like a puppet. I still think of the things he did to me. He taught me every thing I knew sexually. If only he hadn't crossed me, he'd still be alive. And we'd still be in love. I wanted his baby, but he thought it was better if I had the abortion. He said we had plenty of time to have children together, and I believed him. He tricked me, breaking my heart in the process. I could never forgive him for that. Though I would miss him, I knew I had to kill him and my mother, too. It was the only way I would have peace of mind about all I endured.

The next man I loved, Colby Patterson, played me, too. He reminded me so much of my stepdad—the strong, silent-type—a great businessman and a family man. He claimed to have an issue with dating younger women, but I knew when the time was right, I'd have him. Cole knew I loved him, and he took advantage of that. He sexed me, and then chose that other woman over me. That move should've cost him his life, too, but I spared him. He had younger children to look after. Plus, I was convinced that he'd eventually come to his senses and realize that he not only loved me, but he needed me. The bottom line is I got played.

But that Dr. Lawrence Weisman had another thing coming if he thought he was going to use me and then throw me away like yesterday's garbage. It was the doc's job to read me—analyze me. But I always had on my thinking cap, so he'd never outthink me.

Doc had arranged it so that I could have extra time outside the room that housed me daily, but he said he couldn't justify giving me day or even weekend passes, given what I'd done to get myself locked up again. I really couldn't argue with that. I'd done my share of damage on the other side of the mental institution, so I wouldn't trust me either—especially since True Hope was in Atoka, Tennessee, less than an hour away from Memphis and the people I'd given hell to.

Every evening after dinner, a security officer and one of the staff members would come to my room to see if I wanted to do extracurricular activities or just sit out on the patio and watch everyone else play games and such. This day, I only wanted to be a spectator. I had to get my thoughts together for how Doc and I would spend our time the next day. I lay in my bed when the knock came on my door, and then it opened only seconds later.

"What're you gonna do today, Karma?" Julie, a blond-haired, blue-eyed female assistant asked. She was the assistant to Nurse Mitchell.

I reached at the foot of my bed and grabbed the iPod and earplugs Doc ordered me. "I'm going out, but I'm only going to sit on the patio."

Julie nodded then beckoned me to get up. "Let's go."

When I stepped into the hall, I saw Timothy, an armed guard, just outside my door, waiting for us.

"Hey, Tim," I said and flashed him a smile.

"Hey, Karma," he answered simply.

"Oh, Tim, you look like you've been working out in the sun," I said, flirting.

"Behave, Karma," Julie snapped.

"What?" I turned to her. "I'm just calling it like I see it. I mean, the man does have bulging arms and a nice tan to coat them."

"Karma, if you don't stop it, I'm going to escort you right back inside your room. Do you hear me?" The look on Julie's face was serious, so I complied.

"Alright," I said, and with a swiping motion across my lips, I added, "I'm zipping it."

Once outside, I headed to an empty lawn chair and sat down. There wasn't much to look at outdoors. The landscaping was nice—colorful flowers, green shrubbery, artistic garden statues, and an open green field of grass for playing games like volleyball and kickball. But the entire facility was framed by a ten-foot stone wall that would be next to impossible to scale. I knew because I'd gotten close enough to the wall to determine that its creator designed it with the intention of keeping everything on either side of it at bay.

I glanced at the wall then shook my head as I plugged my ears and scrolled through my iPod. Before I could decide what music I wanted to listen to, crazy-ass Teresa Jordan sat next to me and disturbed my peace. I saw her out of my peripheral, so I knew not to look up.

"Hey, Karma," she said.

I tried to ignore her. She didn't know there was no music playing on my iPod yet. I closed my eyes and bounced my head to an imaginary beat, so she could think I was really jamming to a song in my ears. She called me again.

"Hey, Karma."

Still, I ignored her. Unlike me, Teresa was crazy for real. She giggled and talked to her damn-self all the time. I'd seen her trying to feed the air, or who she said was her friend, but there was never anybody in the seat next to her as she dropped food all over everything. The staff would get pissed, too. Teresa would tell them she couldn't help it if her friend was a sloppy eater.

Officer Tim told me Teresa was in for stabbing her neighbor in the back with a fork because her imaginary friend told her the woman cussed her out for no reason. I asked Teresa if that story was true, but she said no. She said everybody just wants her to be psychotic, but she's really not. I laughed because I've heard it time and time again that crazy people will always tell you they're *not* crazy.

I could no longer ignore Teresa once she tapped my shoulder. "Karma," she called again. "Karma."

I opened my eyes and huffed just before pulling the plugs from my ears. "What's up, Tee?"

She giggled. "I like when you call me Tee." She cupped her mouth then giggled some more.

"Yeah, yeah, what can I do for you?"

"I got some cards. I wanted to know if you wanna play cards with me." Even more giggling followed.

I wanted to ask her why everything was so damn funny, but I bit my bottom lip and held back. I noticed Tee didn't do much to her hair. It was pulled back in a ponytail and looked as if she'd just gotten out of the bed without brushing it. Strands were all over the place. I glanced down at the freshly opened deck of red Bicycle brand playing cards in her hand. The torn plastic from the small box was still in the other hand.

She continued. "I was thinking we can play Pluck."

Now I was really frustrated. *She disturbed me for this?* "Tee, we don't even have another player. It takes three people to play Pluck."

Again, more giggling. "Un-huh, yes, we do. We have three players," she said without a doubt. She motioned to the empty space next to her. "Fee-Fee says she wants to play."

I could've screamed. "Fee-Fee? Are you kidding me? She isn't real."

"Oh, yes she is!" The giggling stopped, and Tee seemed mad. "I'm disappointed in you, Karma. I thought you weren't like the rest of 'em. But you're a hater, too."

"Exactly what am I hating on, Tee?"

"My friend—everyone is jealous because my friend came here with me, but they couldn't bring their friends."

I sat back in my chair. "Oh, yeah, right. You're exactly right, Tee. I'm jealous." I was being facetious, but Tee couldn't tell. I shook my head in amazement.

"Her name is Felicia, but I've been calling her Fee-Fee ever since you nicknamed me Tee." The giggle must've been on pause because suddenly it returned.

"Nice," I said then went back to scrolling through my iPod. "Thanks for offering, but I don't want to play no cards, Tee. Maybe you and Fee-Fee should play Go Fish with each other."

I looked up just in time to see her eyes light up. "Heeeeyyy, that's a great idea! Thanks, Karma. We'll just do that." She stood to leave. "Oh, and Fee-Fee and I won't be here this weekend. We've got a pass."

This time *my* eyes lit up. "Oh, yeah? You get weekend passes?"

"Um-hmm, and day passes, too. I get to go see my nanna, and my auntie, and my sister, Josie—whoever's turn it is to check me out."

"Oooohhh," I responded, nodding. Light bulbs went off in my head like dancing Christmas lights. "Well, you have a wonderful time, Tee." I leaned to the other side of her and said, "And you, too, Ms. Fee-Fee. I'll see y'all when you get back, okay?" The smile on my face was as wide as the Mississippi River.

Tee stood, giggling and smiling back, but she had no idea the plans I had. She stood about my height, my weight, my size, and my complexion—oh, it was about to go down.

Lawrence

3

I made it home just after eight o'clock. Aisha knew I would be coming home late and was having dinner out, so imagine my surprise when I was greeted at the front door by a plethora of Asian seasonings flowing from the kitchen. I hadn't replaced the battery in my garage door opener yet, so I had to enter through the living room. I didn't see Aisha posted on the sofa, watching TV as usual, so I headed toward the kitchen to see if she was in there.

I called out to her. "Aisha, baby, I'm home." I didn't get a response, so I called her again. "Aisha!" Still, no answer.

I walked farther into the house and rounded the corner only to discover a lonely kitchen. Aisha left the light on above the stove—possibly so I could see what she cooked. I glanced at the sweet and sour chicken, fried rice and steamed vegetables, neatly covered in Tupperware with clear tops, and then I quickly turned and headed toward the den.

The den was the coziest place for getting into a flick, and my wife loved watching her Lifetime movies on the 60" Panasonic flat screen HD TV.

As I approached the entryway to the den, I could tell she wasn't in there either because it appeared dark and extremely quiet. I took a peek anyway, and just as I'd thought, the room was vacant. I turned and called out to her again.

"Aisha," I said just loud enough to be heard halfway through the house. When she didn't respond, I walked back through the kitchen to peek out into the garage. Her car was there, so I headed toward our bedroom.

She had to be home because her snow-white Lexus was in our three-car garage. We didn't need a garage of that size, but given it was already built with the house, I couldn't complain. We used half of the garage to store our grills and patio furniture in the winter. The other half neatly housed both of our luxury cars.

Our home also was built with two levels, five bedrooms and a bonus room that I used as my office. Three of our four full baths hardly ever got used, but they came into great use whenever the in-laws or any other company were around for a spell. We knew five thousand square feet was a bit much when we bought the home—our second home—only three years ago, but Aisha and I were keen on living in our lavished Collierville neighborhood. We knew it would be a great place to raise children, in the event we ever had them. All of our neighbors were either doctors, lawyers, dentists, or some other six and seven figure professions. Most of them had small children already.

I entered our bedroom, which was dimly lit and pleasantly fluid with soft, sensual jazz. My sweetheart became a huge George Duke fan after hearing "Missing You" at a friend's wedding a year after we met. Stepping into our bedroom to the sweet sounds was no surprise.

Aisha was in the shower. The bathroom door was open, and I could hear the water running, quietly through the thick shower glass walls. I decided to ease over to our California king-sized bed to take a seat and wait for her. Before I could have a seat, I noticed she'd placed a skimpy, two-piece, white negligee on her side of the bed. She had no way of really knowing when I would be home, given I hadn't told her a time, but Aisha always made sure she would be pleasing to my eyes whenever I came home.

When I heard the shower turn off, I stood to undress, so I could jump in next. Aisha stepped out of the bathroom, covered by a towel, and drying her hair with another one. She didn't see me at first because her eyes were closed. I didn't mean to startle her.

"Hey, baby," I said.

She jumped, nearly dropping the towel from her hand. "Oh! Larry, you scared me." She heaved as she spoke.

"I'm sorry, baby. I didn't want to disturb you in the shower. How was your day?"

"It was fine until I got home," she said as she wrapped her hair into the towel.

I continued peeling off my clothes. "What do you mean? What's going on?"

"I don't know, Larry, something weird is going on here. The phone keeps ringing every so often, and the number is coming from the hospital, but no one ever says anything."

"Our home phone?"

"Yes, and the calls have been coming every since I made it home."

"Wait. Did you say they came from the hospital?" I couldn't imagine who we knew in the hospital. "Which hospital, baby?"

"True Hope," she answered matter-of-factly.

I stumbled over my Stacy Adams as I lost focus of what I was doing. I stood, perplexed, in my black socks, white boxers, and my white under shirt. I guess I was silent for so long that Aisha didn't think I'd heard her.

"Hello! Earth to Dr. Lawrence Weisman . . . honey, did you hear what I just said?"

"Huh?" I had to snap out of my shock. "Oh, um, yeah, baby. I heard you." I picked up my clothes and headed toward our dry-clean only laundry bag in the closet. "How many times did the phone ring?"

"I don't know, honey, I lost count. It happened just that many times."

"Are you sure the calls came from True Hope?" I yelled from the closet.

"I'm positive. The caller ID even stated it."

I almost didn't want to leave the closet until I could come up with an excuse that sounded plausible. I walked back into the bedroom anyway. Aisha sat on the bed, smoothing on that sweet-smelling, silky lotion I loved so much on her.

"Well, I don't know, baby. We did have problems with the phones today," I lied. "Maybe the lines malfunctioned in a manner so that they called out when they weren't supposed to. I wonder how many other people had calls from there today."

Aisha frowned. "That can happen? I mean, a business line dialing random numbers?"

"Well, baby, I don't know. I'm just as stumped as you. I'll ask around tomorrow when I get to work."

"Oh, okay. Well, at least the calls seem to have stopped for now."

"I'm going to shower, and when I get back, I want you in that little white number on the bed, looking good for daddy."

Aisha spread that magical smile I loved so much across her face. She didn't have to say anything. Her eyes said it all. She was just as ready for me in bed as I was for her.

When I walked out of the master bath fifteen minutes later, Aisha set her book on the nightstand and beckoned me to her.

"Do you need to go to the kitchen for dinner first, babe, or are you ready for dessert?"

I dropped the towel from my waist, exposing my rock-hard nakedness. "Oh, I'm ready for dessert."

She giggled, and I chuckled a bit, too. She pulled the covers back so I could get a good look at her. To say she was fine would be an understatement. My baby looked amazing. Any color would compliment her complexion, but that white spoke volumes of sex appeal.

"Is this new?" I asked, tugging on the strings that kept her breast enclosed.

"Yes. I was hoping we would sit and have dinner and conversation in our dining room tonight, and then retire to the bedroom for some dessert. You're late, but I guess I should just be thankful I have a man that comes home to me period, huh?"

I stared into her eyes as she lay back on her pillow with one knee raised. I paused because I needed to say the right thing. The truth would devastate her, and she didn't deserve the truth. So, I kissed her softly on the lips before responding.

"I'm so sorry about dinner, baby. I didn't know you would go ahead and cook anyway."

"Well, I had already thawed the chicken, and besides, I had to eat, too, right?"

I released the string on her negligee, exposing her breasts, and then massaging them. "But guess what," I said softly.

"What?"

"I'm the luckiest man in the world to have you." I knew I had gained control of the conversation when she smiled. I continued, "Not every man has a wife so wonderful and dedicated enough to still cook when she knows he won't be home in time. I wouldn't trade you for the world, girl. You hear me?"

"Thank you, honey. I wouldn't trade you either." She leaned closer and placed a slow kiss on my lips.

"And guess what?" I said.

"What?"

"Now I don't have to go out to lunch tomorrow. When I'm done putting you to sleep, I'm going to the kitchen to fix my lunch and clean the remaining dishes."

"You know, you're wonderful, too, honey," Aisha said.

"Thank you, baby."

I silenced her when I slid my tongue into her mouth. She moaned as I caressed her breasts with one hand and fondled between her legs with the other.

I had just stripped the lace fabric from her body and worked my face between her legs when the home phone rang. She rose to answer it, but I pressed her body back to the bed.

"I'm sure it's not important," I said. "We can check the voicemail later."

She nodded, and the phone stopped. As I began my duty of helping her climb to ecstasy, the phone rang again. This time, Aisha was too caught up to try to answer. Each time the phone stopped ringing, the caller would dial again. I must admit the noise was very distracting, but I refused to let it get the best of me.

I knew in all likelihood Karma was up to no good. But what I couldn't understand was how though. How could she get out of her room after 9:00 P.M. to make calls? And how did she get my home number? This meant someone on staff had to be helping her. I needed to get to the bottom of this and fast.

Aisha climaxed back to back. She was spent, and it was a good thing, too, because I needed to leave. I got out of bed, leaving her on her back, trembling and gasping to catch her breath.

"Where're you going, honey? Just give me a second to catch my breath. I'm going to take care of you."

I had glanced at the caller ID and noticed something that nearly took my breath away. Not only had the call come from True Hope, but this time, it came from my office. Aisha turned to me and began rubbing my thigh as I stood gawking at the identifier.

"C'mon, babe. I'm ready," she said.

"Um, Aisha, baby, go ahead and get you some rest. I need to go back to the office."

She nearly popped up from the bed like a Jack-in-the-Box. "What?" I could tell she was irritated as her tone was almost that of a roar. "Tonight? Are you serious?"

"I'm sorry, baby, but I left something." I hurriedly grabbed a T-shirt and some sweat pants from the dresser drawers then started into the bathroom. "I promise I won't be long, okay?"

I closed the bathroom door and stared into the mirror. *Lawrence, man, this is some deep shit you're in now,* I said to myself. It was then obvious to me that Karma was more of a problem than I ever knew she'd be. She wanted war, and there was nothing left to do, but to give it to her.

Karma

4

---

*I*t had to be close to 11:00 P.M. or after when I heard my door opening. I didn't move though. Sometimes the security and nursing staff would randomly check on the rooms and patients, just to ensure everything was fine. I figured this was one of those nights. I was wrong.

"Turn on the lights," he said.

I lay there, thinking I couldn't have heard who I thought it was. Before I could sit up and turn toward the door, the lights flicked on, blinding me a bit. My hand immediately rose to shield my eyes.

"Do you need me to hang in here?" I heard another male voice say. When I took a peek, I saw a short, white, bald guy in the security uniform.

"No," Doc replied. "Just stand outside the door for me."

"Okay," the man said then backed out of the room, closing the door behind him.

I sat in bed, blinking, trying to focus on Doc. I couldn't believe he was really standing in my room.

"Doc? What's going on? Why are you here?"

"You know why I'm here, Karma." He looked angry.

"Um, no. If I knew I wouldn't have asked the question."

"Karma," he said slowly. "You know, at this very moment, I'm starting to question whether I like you anymore."

That hurt. Here I was in bed, minding my own business and anticipating my time with him the next day, but he comes in to awaken me and express sudden disdain for me. His visit made no sense.

"Really, Doc? And why is that?"

As I slid my feet onto the floor, I eased them into my house shoes. I was a little embarrassed to let the doc see me in my hospital pajamas, but there was nothing I could do about that. He took a seat on the side of the bed, next to me.

Staring at the floor, he said, "You play too many games, Karma."

I was taken aback. "Me? Playing games?" I shook my head. I was truly lost. "I'm sorry, Doc, but could you help me out here? I have no idea what's going on or what you're talking about."

He looked into my eyes. "You're really going to sit here and play ignorant, huh?"

I sighed. "Doc, I'm so lost right now, it's ridiculous. I mean, I'm happy to see you—in spite of your attitude— but I really don't know what's going on."

Doc stood. "Get your robe on. We're going to take a walk."

I stood to do as told. My robe hung in the small closet space near my bed. Just after sliding it on, one of the nurses on the night staff entered.

"Sorry, it took me a minute to catch up to you, Dr. Weisman. The call I was on was urgent," she said. "What are we doing?"

"We're going to escort, Ms. Jolley down to my office," he responded.

"Okay," she answered, looking at me. "Should I pull her file?"

"No," he said abruptly. "This won't take long."

Though puzzled, I followed Doc, the nurse, and the security officer down the hall. I couldn't remember the last time I'd been out of my room so late at night. Everything was quiet. I tried to catch up and walk side-by-side with Doc, but his strides were swift and long. Even the nurse and security officer panted as they tried to keep up.

"Why're we going to your office?" I asked.

Doc didn't answer. I assumed it was because he didn't want to talk about much in front of the officer and nurse. My mind began to wonder. Was he having a moment where he wanted to do something exciting and spontaneous with me? I finally caught up to him. He glared straight ahead. His profile was a sight to see. His jaw was tight, and his teeth were clenched. No, he definitely hadn't removed me from my room for anything romantic or sexual. I decided to ask more questions.

"Doc, are we going to counseling?" I waited for a reply but didn't get one. "I mean, I'm just asking since we're heading to your office."

He ignored me again then began drilling the officer.

"What time did you come in?" Doc asked him.

"Oh, I've been here since nine," the officer said.

I hadn't seen this guy before—probably because his shift started after my lock down. Doc continued to question him.

"Did you notice anything strange going on when you came in?"

"No, not at all."

"Were all the patients locked down?"

"Yes, sir—only the nurses walked the halls with other security, passing out meds."

Once we made it to Doc's office, he unlocked the door then asked the officer and nurse to remain outside. He beckoned me in then closed the door before turning on the light. I was flabbergasted by the sight.

"What the hell happened here?" I asked, looking around.

"That's what you're going to tell me, and I mean now!"

"Huh?"

"How the hell did you get into my office?" he snapped.

I stood, probing the room. It was a mess. All of his books were thrown to the floor, bookcases overturned, and paperwork was torn and thrown everywhere. I couldn't believe Doc would automatically point the finger at me.

I stepped closer to him and slid my hand up his chest. "Now, baby, you don't really think I would do something like this, do you?"

He angrily pushed my hand away. "Who else would do this, Karma?"

"I don't know—"

"What? You don't know?"

"Baby, I swear to you—I don't know!"

He clenched his teeth again, and this time, I saw his temple moving along with a thick vein on the side of his head.

"Baby, calm down," I told him.

"Don't you fucking tell me to calm down!" He cut his eyes at me. "I thought we had an understanding."

"Baby, we did. I mean, we do. I didn't do this. You've got to believe me."

"And what am I supposed to tell my boss about what happened here?"

I was at a loss for words. No matter what I said, Doc would not believe I hadn't been in his office since my last visit.

"Who's in cahoots with you?"

"What?"

"There is somebody or some people on this staff in cahoots with you."

"Baby, I swear there is nobody scheming anything with me, and I didn't do this. I know I threatened to cut up, but I swear I had nothing to do with this."

He walked over to his desk then picked up the phone and shook it. "How did you get my home number?"

he asked. I shook my head, and before I could answer, he said, "Don't keep lying to me, Karma, because I will have your li'l ass thrown so far away from here into a prison that you will wonder if you're still located on the map. Stop lying to me, damnit!"

"But I . . . I—"

"Don't you do it," he said. "Don't you fix your lips to give me another lie."

I was frozen solid. It was clear that the only thing Doc wanted to hear was that I did it—that I did everything he accused me of. I couldn't tell him that. He would never get me to say that. I just stared him in the eyes. Neither of us blinked. He stepped so close in my face that I had to close my eyes and open them again to refocus on his.

"I want you to listen to me, and hear me well." He paused, and I swallowed. "No more demands from you. You will *not* threaten me, call my home, nor come into my office when I'm not here and throw tantrums, or else I will start damage control, leaving your ass looking less like a victim and more like the criminal you are. Do I make myself clear?"

When I didn't say anything, his eyes widened, and his eyebrows meshed together. I responded softly, "I hear you."

"Good. Now, I'm going to have the surveillance tapes reviewed, and if I find out who's helping you, things will get ugly from there. In fact, you might just want to let whoever it is know that I said their ass is grass!"

He brushed pass me, knocking into my shoulder. He opened the door then stepped into the hall and called for the officer and nurse.

"Yes, sir?" I heard the officer answer.

"Ms. Jolley is done here. You can escort her back to her room."

"Will do, sir."

Before the officer could meet me at the door, Doc turned to me and said, "Get your *ass* out of my office, and don't call me. I'll call you."

He didn't even look at me. He walked straight to his desk and began straightening things. I stepped out into the hall before the officer could reach me and closed the door behind me.

Doc had just punked me. I couldn't believe it. I had a million thoughts going on in my head, but no words I could say. How had the tables turned? I had him playing out of my hands. He was supposed to operate by my rules. After all, I was the patient. Surely he didn't think I would stand by and let him control me or our relationship. Doc had me twisted, and it would only be a matter of time before I took back my power.

Lawrence

5

*T*he digital clock on my nightstand read 2:04 A.M. by the time I eased back into my bedroom. Aisha was asleep in the middle of the bed. I knew what that meant. She didn't want to miss what time I came in. She shouldn't have been overly concerned because I called her a couple of times from the office, so she'd know I was there. The fact that I'd checked in didn't seem to have any bearing on her mood. She snapped at me and cut me off each time I called.

I undressed then lightly shook Aisha to wake her, so she'd move over and I could climb into bed. I should've thought better of it because she cussed me out in English and Japanese. I let her have her say because I was too tired to argue. Plus, I needed her to get it all out so I could get some sleep. I still had to be at work by eight in the morning.

It wasn't until we sat at the breakfast table in the kitchen together that I'd had enough of her lashing at me.

"And, Larry, I don't know who you think I am," she said in the middle of her tirade. "I'm not going to be a push over for you. You aren't going to treat me this way!"

I slammed my fist on the table. "What way? Huh? How am I treating you, Aisha? Hell, I went to work! I called you from my office. What do you think I was doing at True Hope till after one? Huh?"

"Oh, I don't know! Maybe you had somebody meet you there."

"Somebody like who? What are you saying, Aisha? Just come out and say what's on your mind!"

She yelled to the top of her lungs. "Are you fucking around on me?"

There. She let it out. Now I was stumped, and I wasn't sure why. I knew she had wanted to ask it, but I wasn't prepared to answer her. We stared into each other's eyes. When I didn't respond immediately, Aisha's slanted, dark eyes threatened me with tears.

"Oh, baby, don't," I said, waving across the table at her. "Baby, don't cry. C'mere." I slid back my chair and beckoned her over. "C'mere, baby."

She came over, sat on my lap, and buried her head into my neck. "I don't think I can handle knowing if you are—"

"Aisha, baby, listen. You don't have to worry about that. We're good, okay?" I didn't know what else to say.

When she produced hot tears onto my neck, I hated myself. I could tell she knew something was going on, but as she'd said, she didn't want to face it. Aisha didn't deserve to be mistreated, nor did I intend to abuse her in any way. I just found Karma challenging and interesting. I never imagined messing around with her would bring about so much drama. Aisha sat up and wiped her tears. I took my unused napkin from the table to help her.

"I don't like the way I'm feeling, Larry. I used to feel secure."

"You do know that I love you, right?"

She sighed. "Yes, but—"

"Ssshhh," I said, placing my finger to her lips. "There's no 'but', baby. You hear me?"

"Larry—"

"Un-un. Listen to me, Aisha." I paused, looking into her saddened, wet, red eyes. "You're the one I married, and nothing or no one is going to come between us. Okay?"

"Larry, I hope you're not asking me to be number one, knowing there is a number two."

I shook my head. "Of course not, baby. I would never ask you to do that."

"Then, what are you saying?"

I swallowed hard, remembering she had just said she couldn't handle knowing the truth. I didn't want to hurt her any more than she was already. I placed a soft kiss on her lips before answering.

"I'm saying that I can see I've clearly hurt you. And I'm sorry. I'm going to work on keeping you happy from now on."

She dropped her head and collapsed onto my shoulder, releasing more tears. She knew. I said it without saying it—that was my confession. But I needed her to understand that I was done with my mess. I tried to lift her from my shoulder.

"Baby, listen," I said, pulling on her. She gripped my neck even tighter as she continued to cry. "Listen, baby. I'm sorry, okay? We're going to be fine. I promise. I need for you to believe me. I love you, Aisha."

Aisha sobbed until she seemed to be just plain tired. She kept her head buried in my neck for what seemed like an hour. I was running late for work, but I didn't care. I couldn't leave my wife in that state.

I had my work cut out for me. I needed to make Aisha feel secure in our marriage again, and I needed to figure out a way to get rid of Karma.

I led Aisha back to the bedroom and made love to her like I should have the night before. Although her eyes were filled with sorrow, she gave me all of her. She made love right back to me as though nothing ever vexed her spirit that morning.

I was an hour and a half late for work. I had cleaned up most of the damage to my office the night before, but I still had books that needed to be placed back onto the shelves. Steve walked into my office and did a double-take.

"Yo', Dr. Weisman, are you moving? What's up with all the books stacked everywhere?"

"Guess," I said simply as I pecked away on my keyboard.

I looked up in time to see Steve shake his head in confusion. "Um, you're about to donate them to charity or what?"

"No, guess again."

"I really don't know. If you're not changing offices, I have no idea what's going on?" He took a seat in the chair in front of my desk.

I stopped typing long enough to enlighten him. "There was a storm last night, and it's still brewing this ol' way."

"Huh?" Steve shook his head and laughed.

"Yeah, somebody needs to laugh because I sure as hell can't."

"Why not?"

I stared him right in the face. "The storm's name is Hurricane Karma."

"Oh, snap! Tell me you're lying!"

"I wish I could." I shook my head. "I'm typing up some papers now. That bitch has got to go."

"My man! Now you're talking."

"You know she's sane, right?"

"How do you figure?"

"Oh, she's cunning, conniving, and a criminal alright. But one 'C' word she isn't—crazy."

"I know I'm not her doctor, but I believe she's definitely schizophrenic, Lawrence. She's got too many characteristics."

"Be that it may, but for the purposes of getting her ass out of here, I'm writing that the bitch is sane."

Steve shook his head. "Lawrence, be careful, man. You don't want to state that she's sane and send her to prison where she could cause harm to somebody else."

"I'm just expressing my professional opinion."

"Yeah, but it's an opinion that has two sides. You can't honestly tell me that in your heart of hearts you don't believe that girl has some real mental issues."

"She's bitter, hateful, and yeah, sometimes delusional—"

"And there you have it . . . send her to another facility, but don't deny her the adequate help she needs."

"So, I'm guessing you're insinuating I never gave her professional help."

"That I cannot say, but I would say perhaps her time with you hasn't been as efficient as it could have been had neither of you crossed the lines."

What could I say? There was no denying that I was as wrong as two left shoes about having sex with Karma. I had no intentions of continuing though. How the affair started didn't matter at this point. All that mattered was how to put a stop to all the inappropriate behavior on both of our parts. I needed Steve's help.

"You're right. And I'm done with all the madness, but I'm going to need your help."

"What's up?"

"I'll rewrite the paperwork, but it's going to take some time to get her transferred. Will you take her on as your patient?"

"'H' to the 'E' to the double 'L' 'L'! Hell naw, man, and you knew not to even fix your mouth to ask me anything like that."

Steve stood as if he was about to leave. I panicked and stood also. I walked over to him in front of my desk.

"C'mon, Steve. You said yourself I needed to find a way to get rid of her. I can't be her doctor, given the circumstances. Plus, she's got somebody on staff working with her."

Steve was in the middle of shaking his head, rendering me no for an answer until I said the last part about someone on staff working with her.

"You want to run that by me again?" he stated.

"I can't see any other way she could make the calls to my home and from my office after hours. My office was still locked when I came to check on it. So, if it wasn't broken into, how did she get in here?"

"That's a good question. Did you check the surveillance cameras?"

"I've sent a request to the head of security to view the tapes, but I haven't gotten a response yet."

"I can't believe what I'm hearing right now. The plot just keeps thickening. Who in the world would be teaming with her against you?"

"I don't know, but I hope those videos will let me know."

"Yeah, me, too," Steve said as he turned to leave.

"You never answered my question."

"What question?"

"Can I have her referred to you?"

"Oh, I answered your question. Can't you spell? I said 'H' to—"

"Look, man, just think about it."

"Um, yeah . . . how about I pray about it?"

"Since when did you start praying or even begin a relationship with God?"

"I haven't," he said as he opened the door. "But maybe this is a good time to start for a friend." He laughed.

"C'mon, Steve, this is serious."

"I know, but Barbara does all the praying in our house. That woman is in church more hours out of the day than she's home."

"I hear you, but I don't want your wife in this. I have enough problems with my own woman as it is. I don't need to be trying to explain anything to yours, too."

He hurriedly closed the door and stepped back over to me. "You told Aisha?"

"Not exactly. After last night, we had problems, so she knows I haven't been totally honest—nor faithful, but she doesn't know who or how."

Steve shook his head. "Oh, I was just about to ask if you were crazy. I hope you two be okay, but don't you be fool enough to tell her who or what you've been doing, Lawrence."

"You don't even have to advise me of that. I still have a little sense."

"Good, so use it and keep your dick in your pants until we can figure out how to get this girl off your back." He started toward the door again.

"You do mean 'we', don't you?"

He stopped then turned and said, "Yeah, but don't get too excited, and don't put in that request for transfer yet." He sighed. "I need some time to figure out a plan of action and how to write up that request for extended treatment in another facility. I don't plan to have her under my care for long."

"Oh, Steve, man, I owe you."

"You sure in the hell do! It may cost you dearly, but I'll make sure you and Aisha can still live comfortably." He chuckled on his way out the door.

I knew Karma would be pissed once I had her transferred into Steve's care, but that didn't worry me in the least. I planned to work feverishly with Steve on getting her out of our facility all together. Karma had become too much for me to handle. She had Steve to thank for me not having her sent to prison just yet. Now all I had to do was keep her under control until her psychiatrist could be renamed. But as I sat at my desk thinking of all of this, something told me I was in for a rude awakening.

Karma

6

So, I made a new friend. It was not my intention, but Teresa came with benefits I couldn't afford to turn away. Ever since she told me about her passes out of the facility, I couldn't stop thinking of ways I could convince her to let me use them from time to time. I could pretend to be her once she checked out. We just needed to figure out the details of who would check her out, and how the swap would be made, considering she'd have to stay in my room until I could return.

The idea was to be able to spend time with Doc outside of the nuthouse, but that would take a minute before that could happen. He was still mad at me. He told me to wait until he called *me*, which was very hard for me to do, but I did as told. No sense in making him any angrier than he was already. I'd never seen him so upset, and for what? Sure, I could snap when I get ready, but Doc hadn't seen that side of me. I just couldn't understand why he would automatically assume I was the one who trashed his office.

It had been exactly ten days since I'd last heard from Doc. He really was trying my patience. I didn't like giving him the upper hand like that, but what he failed to realize was that I was the master strategist. The more time he gave me, the better I could plan. I had a number of wild thoughts running through my mind—most of them he would like.

Perhaps Doc didn't understand after all—he made me feel things Colby never made me feel. He was from the hood—I looked him up. I had to know where that rugged side of him came from. He was intelligent, but every now and then, he'd display a side that let me know he was a rough neck. Shoot, it wouldn't surprise me if he was once a dope boy. He could have a hard exterior when necessary—hence the way he treated me in his office the other week. He made me out to be guilty regardless of what I tried to say, and if we weren't in his office, I might've run, fearing for my safety. He had a look that said he didn't play.

While he had me on punishment, Teresa and I became more and more chummy. I even obliged her in a game of cards each day. My only issue was listening to her talk about that damn Fee-Fee.

"Fee-Fee told me she was really glad you're our friend now," Tee said as we sat on the back lawn, playing Go Fish.

"Yeah, well I prefer if she stay away, but since she's your friend, I put up with her," I said just before calling another card. "Give me all your eights."

"Go fish," Tee responded, poking her lip. "What did Fee-Fee ever do to you?"

"She talks too much. You know I don't like to be asked a lot of questions." I straightened my hand of cards. "Your turn. Call a card."

"Um." She stared at her cards. "Give me all your fives."

"Go fish."

Tee pulled from the deck on the small table between us then straightened her hand. "Well, I guess I could ask her not to talk so much around you. Would that help?"

"Yes . . . please do. That would help me to like her much better." I giggled inside. "Now give me all of your threes."

I watched Tee scan her eyes over her cards, and then her expression lit up like a Jack-o-lantern. Tee pulled out two sets of threes and gave them to me.

"I win!" she screamed.

"What the—" I almost lost it. "Tee, you had two pairs of threes all this time?"

"Yup!" Her awkward giggle paid us a visit.

"So, why didn't you play them before now?"

"'Cause I knew you'd need them!" She giggled again.

I sighed. "I quit. I don't want to play anymore. The more I teach you, the dumber I get."

"Why? You shouldn't get mad, Karma. I let you win sometimes."

As she sat there with a stupid grin on her face, I wanted to give her a back-and-forth slap like Moe did Curly on the Three Stooges. Some people you can't be nice to. She irked the hell out of me—just because—but damn, she had something I really needed. I swallowed my pride and remained kind.

"I'm not mad, Tee. I'm just tired. How about you play with Fee-Fee for a while? I think she's getting a little jealous that you've been spending so much time with me."

"Oh, okay. I think you're right."

"Hey, look. There's an empty table over there. It's shaded, too. You should take Fee-Fee over there and spend some quality time with her."

"Okay. You sure you won't be mad?"

I wanted to say, "Hell naw! Hurry and take your ass on!" But I didn't. Instead, I just shook my head then said, "Oh, I'm positive. I'll be just fine. We can play again tomorrow."

"Well, alright." She turned to her left side. "C'mon, Fee-Fee. We still have time to play before we have to go in for the evening."

As she got up, talking to her imaginary friend along the way, I couldn't do anything but shake my head. That child was more than a little off. She was straight up gone in the head. And they called *me* crazy. At least I've never had imaginary friends. As I lay back in my lawn chair to rest my eyes, I heard a familiar voice, and it was rather friendly this time.

"Ready to get back to your room, Jolley?"

I opened my eyes and sat up. "Nurse Mitchell, how are you doing?"

She looked a few pounds lighter and a couple of shades bronzer than I remembered, but she looked great.

"I'm good. I'm well-rested as a matter of fact." She took a seat on the lawn chair Tee had been sitting on.

"Yeah, I hear you've been on vacation. That must've been nice."

"Mm-hmm. I had a Caribbean vacation—St. Thomas, the U.S. Virgin Islands, Barbados and more! It was a cruise."

"Oh, that sounds like a lot of fun. I've never been to Barbados or on a cruise. I hear once you've experienced life on a ship, you don't want to leave."

"Yes, it was pretty nice."

"So, did you go with your man?"

I don't know what made me ask. I had told myself not to get too close to the staff at True Hope, especially Nurse Mitchell. There was just something about her that made me want to keep my distance. Plus, I didn't want her becoming overly concerned about me. I had to guard my secret relationship from people like her. If Nurse Mitchell knew what Doc and I were doing, everything would come to a halt. She stuttered as she tried to answer the question.

"Um . . . I . . . um—"

"You don't have to answer that," I said, interrupting her. "I apologize. I didn't mean to be nosey."

She smiled. I think that was the first real smile I'd seen on her the entire time I'd been housed there.

"Oh, it's no problem. It's not a secret. It was actually a girlfriend's trip. We were celebrating our twenty-five-year class reunion."

"Wow, from high school?"

"Yes. Can you believe it?"

I shook my head. "No, I can't. You look great!"

She smiled again. "Thanks, Karma. Listen, I just came over to speak before I leave. I'm not officially back until tomorrow. I wanted to see what I have on my plate when I get back."

"Well, don't worry about me. I won't give you no trouble. I've been minding my business for a while now."

"I heard you have. That's good. I'm proud of you."

"I told you: I know how to act when I get ready."

"I agree. Oh, by the way, I see you haven't had a visit with Dr. Weisman in a minute. Nobody can seem to tell me what that's about. You haven't gotten into any mischief, have you?"

"Mischief? Who me?"

She gave me a knowing look, raising an eyebrow. "Yes, you. What have you done?"

"Nurse Mitchell, what makes you think I've done something? I told you I've been minding my own business."

"Is that before or after you cut up?" She placed her hands on hips.

I laughed. "Nurse Mitchell, I have not cut up since you've been off."

"Karma, doctors don't take patients off the schedule unless they've had some type of problem with them."

"I swear—I didn't do anything," I said, raising my right hand. "I've been wondering what's going on myself."

"Hmm. Well, no one else seems to know."

I shrugged. "I know, right? I've tried to find out when I could visit the doc again, but nobody could seem to tell me what's going on either. Perhaps you can ask the doc when you get in tomorrow."

"Um, no. There's really no need. You're scheduled to see him after lunch tomorrow. I guess he just needed to get caught up on some things. I'm glad to hear it was nothing you did."

"Nurse, Mitchell, I could be offended, you know, but since it's you, I won't take your comments to heart," I teased.

"Jolley, you're as hard as a brick. Nothing I say could hurt your feelings." She chuckled as she walked off.

"See ya tomorrow," I yelled to her.

She waved over her shoulder. My evening had taken a turn for the better. Nurse, Mitchell not only stopped by looking good and seemingly feeling great, but she also gave me the best news I'd had in a while. I was scheduled to visit with my boo the next day.

Lawrence

7

Several days went by since I had last seen or even spoken to Karma. If I had my way, I wouldn't have scheduled her for another visit period. In fact, I would've just kept her off the books and bought myself some time until her transfer could be completed. The girl was trouble. She'd recently made my life a living hell. My wife was on alert every time the house phone rang, running to answer it as if she was expecting a winning call from Publisher's Clearing House Sweepstakes. Karma hadn't called my house anymore, but Aisha was still on guard, and she didn't want me going anywhere after work hours without her.

I wasn't looking forward to a meeting with Karma, but I knew it had to be done before people became suspicious. It would have been eleven days that I hadn't met with her had I not scheduled a visit. The hour was drawing near till time for her to show up. What could we possibly talk about in an hour? I needed time fillers, so I went on the Internet and found some exercises and questionnaires for her to do. She could sit at my desk and work online. I anticipated the exercises to take up twenty minutes each, which would be our entire meeting by the time she was done.

When I heard the small knock on the door, my heart skipped a nervous beat. "Come in," I stated.

Nurse Mitchell and security escorted Karma in, but she stood near the door until the nurse offered her a seat.

"Go ahead and sit down, Jolley," the nurse said as she walked over to my desk and handed me a folder. "How are you today, Dr. Weisman?"

"I'm fine. Thanks for asking. How are you?"

"Doing fine as well," she stated just before turning to leave. "Is there anything else I can do before I step out?" she asked over her shoulder.

"Um, no. I'll be in touch just before the hour is up. Thanks, Nurse Mitchell."

She and the officer walked out of my office and closed the door. I locked eyes with Karma. She was extremely quiet. I didn't know what to make of her silence.

"Karma," I said then paused. "Are you okay?"

She nodded. "I'm fine."

A hush came over the room. Soon the silence was just plain awkward. I was sure her silence was some type of game for her, but being the psychiatrist that I am, I decided to play along with her. It was my move.

"Well, Karma, it's been a while, and we've got a lot to catch up on in this hour, so we can just go ahead and get started."

"Cool," was all she said.

I wasn't used to this woman. She clearly wanted some type of reaction out of me, but I was careful not to let her read me.

"Okay. I need for you to sit at my desk, if you don't mind. There are some online activities I need for you to complete in this hour."

"And what if I say I mind?" She sat with her legs crossed, swinging the top leg back and forth.

"Well, just in case you're wondering: There's nothing complex about the exercises. We can actually work them together, if you'd like."

She stood and smiled. "Now you're talking."

She started toward my desk, so I stood and slid back my chair for her to sit in. As soon as she got close enough, she caught me by surprise. She quickly grabbed a fistful of my crotch, gripping it just enough to put me in fear of moving.

I squeezed her hand, hoping with enough force to make her stop, but she didn't. I couldn't even pry her hand from me. She was strong—stronger than I had imagined. I panted in fear of what she would do next.

"Karma, what are you doing?" I whispered. She had created just enough pressure to keep me from making rash decisions.

She began unbuckling my pants with the other hand. "I'm claiming what's mine," she answered.

I put up as much resistance as I could without her hurting me, but it was no use. My pants had come down before I knew it. My next thought was that at least she couldn't get an erection out of me. But I was wrong. Karma snatched my boxers down and dropped to her knees quicker than I'd ever seen anyone move.

I'd never had to beg a woman not to suck me off before. This was a first. As I gripped her head and tried to back away, the feeling of her warm, wet tongue stroking me over and over again sent shock waves of ecstasy through my body. I tried to back away again and fell back into my chair. Karma followed, maintaining her erotic pace as she handled me like I'd never been handled before.

She backed under my desk and pulled me to her. I grew longer and harder by the second as she relentlessly took all of me. I heaved uncontrollably. Then my eyes grew large. *The door*, I thought, glancing in its direction. *It's not locked!*

Just as I'd feared, there was one knock right before it quickly swung open. It was Nurse Mitchell, and Karma refused to stop.

"Dr. Weisman," she said then stopped abruptly at the door.

"Um, yes, how may I help you?" I asked as calmly as I could.

Nurse Mitchell had a puzzled look on her face. She glanced around the room, seemingly at a complete loss. The front side of my desk was shielded with the same style of wood as the desktop, and it was a good thing because Karma was underneath, still hard at work. I needed the nurse out of there as quick as possible.

"Ms. Mitchell," I called. "Is there something I can do for you?"

She tilted her head and frowned. "What happened to Jolley?"

I must've looked like a deer in headlights. I knew the lie I wanted to tell, but trying to maintain my breathing while I talked proved to be difficult. I opened my mouth a time or two to speak, but I was afraid to let out a sound. I just stared at the nurse.

Her eyebrows rose. "Dr. Weisman?"

I propped my fist under my chin then answered, "Huh?" That was the best I could do.

"Jolley . . . is she still here?"

I had to gather my composure as best I could. "Oh, um, she," I stammered, pointing. "The restroom. She went to the restroom."

"Oh, well here."

I nearly had a heart attack when the nurse started toward my desk.

"HUH? Um, what's this?" I asked, taking a slip of paper as she handed it to me.

At that moment, Karma relaxed her throat and took all of me again. I inhaled deeply and did my best to release the air slow. My mind wanted her to stop the blissful torture, but my body declared more. This was the best kind of suffering I'd ever endured. I didn't realize I had zoned out the nurse for a few seconds.

"Dr. Weisman, did you hear me?"

"Oh, yes, yes," I lied, blinking at the slip of paper.

"So, just let her know that since she had questions about her meds, I pulled a history of everything she's ever taken and you two can decide which ones you want her to keep taking."

"Great, great. Good deal."

"Thank you, Dr. Weisman," she said as she turned to leave. "Sorry to interrupt."

"Not a problem."

As soon as she walked out and closed the door, I exhaled loudly, and then immediately took in several more breaths and puffed them out. I felt like I was about to explode. I gripped the back of Karma's head and thrust my hips fast and hard. I wanted to release. I needed to erupt. And I did. She savored every drop.

I sat there, panting and sucking in as much air as I could. When I looked down at Karma, she was sitting underneath my desk Indian-style, smiling up at me while tracing my wetness across her lips. I glanced up at the door then jumped up, holding my pants at my waist. I hurriedly locked the door then turned around. Karma was still tucked underneath my desk.

"Get up," I yelled to Karma.

She rose slowly then sat on my desk. "Why? Didn't you enjoy that?"

I walked back over to my desk then tried to remove her. I placed my hands at her hips and attempted to slide her off. "Get down—now!" I used so much force we both almost stumbled.

"Damn, Doc. It's like that now?"

"Like what?"

"You owe me," she said matter-of-factly. "You've never let me leave here without returning the favor."

She slid back up my desk and spread her legs for me to see all of her goods. As usual, she wasn't wearing panties.

"I ordered that hair remover like you suggested a while back," she said atop my desk, spread eagle. "What do you think?"

She took her fingers and massaged herself, increasing my visibility of her gaping hole. I was totally turned on—again. She pointed her index finger then beckoned me. I knew I needed to turn her away, but she looked delectable as she lay back on her forearms rolling her hips toward me. Before I knew it, I had gone in for a taste of her sweet nectar.

Karma held my head and did a slow grind into my face. I was so turned on, I lost all sense of where I was, lost track of time, and was just lost period.

When she reached her climax, it was intense—almost as forceful as mine—the first time. The second time I got off was shortly after I climbed on top of the desk and banged her into submission. The computer's flat-screen monitor shook as I gave her pounding thrusts. She bit her bottom lip and took my wrath until I was done.

I climbed down and sat dazed as she headed into the restroom to wash up. When she stepped out, her hair and clothes were intact. I pulled myself together then called for her to be escorted back to her room.

She sat on the sofa as she waited. Neither of us said anything, but I could see on her face that she thought she'd won. She clearly came with a game plan, and I fell for it.

The knock came, but I didn't move. Karma walked over to the door and quietly unlocked it just before opening it. To my surprise, in walked Steve. He seemed a bit taken aback as he stood in place, glaring at Karma's smirk. I dropped my head as he gawked at me, sitting at my desk.

Not long after that, security walked in and asked Karma if she was ready to go. She nodded then waved goodbye just before vanishing my office. Steve walked over and closed the door. He turned and looked at me for what seemed like minutes, but I know it was only seconds. He finally mustered something to say, and I'll never forget his words.

"You sorry-ass sucker! You fucked her, didn't you?"

I sat behind my desk with my hand under my chin. There was nothing I could say.

Karma

8

D oc should have known I'd come with a plan he wouldn't expect. I imagined his intent was to have a regular, boring session, but our sessions hadn't been regular or boring since day one, and we weren't about to start now. He gave me what I came for, and I went back to my room a happy woman. I thought of Doc all night long. I could only imagine he had me on his brain, too.

The next day was my library day. At 1:00 P.M., I was given an hour on the computer to do whatever I wanted as long as it was within the hospital guidelines. I was not to order anything without permission, no perusing sites about drugs and alcohol, no porn—as if I could actually access those sites, given they were all blocked—and oh, I was not to try to reach Cole, his wife, my daughter, or anyone else who requested no contact from me. Who really wants to contact those people anyway? My daughter would be the only interest for touching base with anyone surrounding her, but at the moment, I had other things on my mind.

I wanted to do what I loved doing most with my time in the computer room — write on my blog. The petite, thin, dark-skinned librarian, who looked to be near retirement age, followed me into the small, closet-like room. She issued me another shocking rule.

"There will be no accessing blogs or any other social media this week, Karma."

My eyes damn near popped out of my head. "Why not?" I snapped.

"That's the new rule until further notice."

"What? But . . . who . . . I don't understand." I glanced over at the other two people in the room. They seemed to be playing some type of games as I noticed their monitors. I shook my head in disbelief. "Is this new rule just for me or for everyone?"

"I don't know if it's just for you or not, but Dr. Weisman specifically told me not to let you have that access."

I should have known Doc had something to do with this new rule. He still didn't trust me. What in the world would I do for an hour without my blog? I wasn't interested in playing games. I had no money on my account to shop, so I needed to think of something else to fill my time in the computer room.

The librarian stood close behind me as I took a seat in front of the 15" flat screen monitor. I turned it on and waited as it uploaded. I glanced over my shoulder a few times, hoping she'd get the hint that she could leave, but she stayed put. I was beyond annoyed.

"So, you have to stand here and watch me, too?" I turned and asked.

She smacked her lips and huffed before answering. "No, but you listen to me, Karma. I'm going to leave you in here alone, but if I find out you accessed those sites, I will see to it that you are banned from the computer room for good."

"Fine," I answered abruptly. "I just don't want you standing over me."

She rolled her eyes then exited the room. She left the door cracked—for what I didn't know. It wasn't like there was a lock on it. She could open it and come in any time she wanted. I went over and closed the door, hoping she wouldn't return to pick on me about me doing so. As I sat back down at my seat, the computer was fully loaded.

My blog was associated with my Write Rest account. I contemplated whether to sneak on to the site. Ultimately, I decided not to. I was sure Doc had told the librarian which site to look out for. I had no doubt he would check behind me, given the entry dates always told when the last post was created. It would take me some time to figure how to outsmart him. Meanwhile, I needed to go to another site he hadn't been watching—eLovers Row.

I had only been on eLovers Row a couple of times, so I knew Doc shouldn't know anything about that site. It was a site for people online to meet people for hookup. My profile pic was an Avatar that closely resembled me. I fixed the Avatar up in a sexy nurse's uniform—cleavage, short skirt and high heels—and the guys I had a chance to chat with loved it.

I logged on to eLovers Row, inputting my screen name, TrueRedKarma. It wasn't long before a couple of guys requested to chat with me. Before I responded, I jumped up to peep out the door. I wanted to see if the librarian was nearby. When I spotted her, she was sitting behind the desk, preoccupied with a phone call. I eased the door shut once again then returned to my seat. When I returned, I saw there was only one guy remaining to chat. I accepted his request.

HI, WANNA CHAT? I'M WHITEKNIGHT42, he typed.

His profile picture was sexy as hell. He had dark hair, an olive complexion and a squared jaw line. The Eiffel Tower was in his background. That really piqued my curiosity.

I CAN SEE THAT IN YOUR SCREEN NAME, HANDSOME, I responded. I CAN ALSO SEE IN YOUR PROFILE THAT YOU'RE 6'2. I LIKE THAT.

He typed back quickly. MY HEIGHT HAS ITS ADVANTAGES.

OH REALLY? WELL, I'D LOVE TO HEAR ABOUT THAT SOMETIME.

YOU GOT TIME NOW, SWEETHEART?

NOT EXACTLY, BUT I PLAN TO MAKE TIME FOR YOU REAL SOON.

CAN I HOLD YOU TO THAT?

ABSOLUTELY.

GREAT BECAUSE YOUR PROFILE SEEMS INTERESTING. I'D LOVE TO SEE A PIC OF YOU, TOO.

IN TIME. SPEAKING OF PICS. YOURS LOOKS INTERESTING. DO YOU LIVE IN PARIS?

He typed a smiley face before responding. NO, SWEETHEART. I WAS ONLY VISITING. I LIVE IN LONDON.

WOW, THAT'S JUST AS FASCINATING.

YOU'VE NEVER BEEN TO LONDON?

NO, I HAVEN'T.

WELL, MAYBE AFTER WE GET TO KNOW EACH OTHER A BIT, I COULD SEND FOR YOU.

SEND FOR ME?

YES. ON MY PRIVATE PLANE.

I was taken aback. Could this man be telling the truth? I began combing through his pictures. I saw photos of him with two young, white women on each side of him. I saw a couple of pictures with him standing near a small plane, and I also saw pictures of him sitting on the plane, enjoying what looked like champagne and hors d'oeuvres.

I guess I had taken a while because he typed, STILL THERE?

YES. I'M HERE. WHAT DO YOU DO FOR A LIVING?

WE CAN DISCUSS THAT IN DETAIL ONCE I GET TO KNOW YOU.

FAIR ENOUGH.

SO HAVE YOU EVER DATED OUTSIDE YOUR RACE?

NO, BUT YOU CERTAINLY CAN BE MY FIRST.

SWEETHEART, I'M SURE I'LL BE YOUR FIRST AND YOUR ONLY.

IS THAT RIGHT?

THAT'S RIGHT. I AIM TO PLEASE.

THEN WHY ARE YOU SINGLE AND ON THIS SITE?

LOOKING FOR YOU.

WHO AM I? I couldn't wait to see how he would answer.

ACCORDING TO YOUR PROFILE, YOU'RE NOT ONLY INTELLIGENT, BUT WHEN IN A RELATIONSHIP, YOU'RE COMMITTED, SPONTANEOUS, AND YOU LOVE HARD. MY KIND OF GIRL. WHAT I SHOULD'VE BEEN LOOKING FOR ALL ALONG.

Oh he was quick on his feet. I liked him. I had one more question for him. THE 42 IN YOUR SCREEN NAME IS YOUR AGE, RIGHT?

SURE IS, SWEETHEART.

AGE DIFFERENCE DOESN'T BOTHER YOU? I found myself almost praying he'd say no.

NOT AT ALL, he answered quickly.

THEN YOU'RE MY KIND OF GUY.

GLAD TO HEAR THAT.

The door opened slightly, and the librarian paused to talk with someone on the other side before entering.

"What do you want now?" I heard her ask the person.

"Is it my turn to get on the computer yet?" I heard a male voice ask.

"No, Mr. Brooks. Go back to the table you were at and have a seat. I'll come get you when it's your turn."

"But—"

The man's voice faded as I returned my attention to the chat. I needed to get WhiteKnight off the screen and click on several more sites before the librarian walked over to view my web history. I typed fast.

SORRY TO END THIS SO ABRUPTLY BUT I HAVE TO GO.

SO SOON? BUT WE WERE JUST WARMING UP. ☺

I KNOW, BUT I'M AT THE DOCTOR'S OFFICE, AND HE'S CALLING ME TO THE BACK NOW.

DOCTOR'S OFFICE? ARE YOU OKAY?

Oh, stop with the chatting already! I just wanted WhiteKnight to say goodbye and be done.

I'M FINE. ROUTINE CHECKUP.

OK. WHEN WILL I HEAR FROM YOU AGAIN?

SOON.

HOW SOON?

SOON. BYE

I hated to do it, but I logged off without a pleasant goodbye. I knew people lied all the time on those sites. Hell, I was one of them. But this WhiteKnight guy had me intrigued.

I pulled up at least ten sites in less than a minute. The librarian was still at the door, trying to get old man, Mr. Brooks, to have a seat. I was glad for that because a minute was all I needed to click on Amazon.com, a few designer fashion sites, eBay, and Bible Gateway among other things. The librarian walked right pass the others in the room and headed straight for me.

"Are you behaving yourself, Karma?" she asked.

"Yes, ma'am."

I turned my head and rolled my eyes. I never knew the woman's name. She didn't wear a name tag, but whoever she was, she got on my last nerve.

"Let me see. Slide over," she said, almost pushing me out of the way as she pulled up a chair.

I rolled my chair over a bit to let her have her way. She quickly pulled up my history, and to my surprise eLovers Row was still listed toward the bottom. As she placed the cursor toward the top of the most recent visited sites, she stopped on a link and turned to me.

"Really, Karma? Bible Gateway?" She twisted her lips.

"And," I snapped. "What's wrong with that? Did Dr. Weisman give orders for me not to visit there either?"

"No, that's not what I'm saying. I'm just curious as to when you get so spiritual."

"When you told me I couldn't visit any social media sites," I quipped.

"Yeah, right, and what scripture did you study?"

Damn, I had to think fast. "The Lord is my shepherd; I shall not want. Psalms 23:1—King James Version." It was one of the first scriptures I learned as a kid, but she didn't have to know that.

She twisted her lips again and replied, "You're a smart aleck, you know that?"

"Now that you've told me so, yes, I do."

She rolled her eyes then gave her focus back to the web history. I drew in a deep breath then exhaled because I knew as soon as she spotted eLovers Row, I was in for an argument. I thought of WhiteKnight and how if this woman banned me from the computer room, I'd never get to chat with him again. I wished there was something I could do to distract her. I started chatting.

"Are you familiar with Psalms 23, Miss?"

She looked at me then rolled her eyes again before answering. "How old do I look to you?"

"Um, I don't think I want to answer that."

She placed her fist on her hip. "I'm sixty-one years old—of course I'm familiar with the Twenty-third Psalm."

"Oh, okay. I just had to ask because not everyone is brought up in a Christian home, you know."

"Karma, leave me alone while I look at this," she said, pointing at the computer screen. "We can talk later, okay?"

This time, I wanted to be the one to roll my eyes, but I answered politely instead. "Okay."

As soon as she glanced back at the screen, the door flung open. It was Mr. Brooks. He was livid.

"You said you would come and get me, dammit!" he yelled, pointing at the librarian.

She jumped up nearly knocking over her chair. "You listen to me, Mr. Brooks! I'm not going to have this out of you today."

She walked over to him at the door, fussing along the way. She paused for a moment to tell me a thing or two.

"Karma, you hurry up with what you're doing on that computer—be it scripture or whatever. I'm cutting everyone's time short today."

The others in the room along with me grunted. I also smiled inside because she was on her way out of the room, and she hadn't discovered my little web secret. I figured now was the time to thank God for small favors.

Lawrence

9

---

*N*ineteen days and counting. That's how long it had been since I'd last seen Karma. I'd been numbering the days on a calendar like a pregnant woman anticipating her due date. If only I had a due date, it would simplify my life. I intentionally avoided scheduling Karma, hoping I would hear back from the board on the approval of her transfer. The plan was to have her transferred before I'd ever have to see her again.

My good friend, Steve, wasn't talking to me—well, at least not much. He'd speak to me in passing, but that was just about it. I know I disappointed him. I just wished he could walk a mile in my shoes, so perhaps he'd understand my dilemma. I shouldn't wish Karma on my worst enemy—let alone Steve. That's why I couldn't help but understand his hesitation in taking her on as his patient. The only thing I could do for now was await a response from the board.

I couldn't keep screwing that woman. The more I sexed her, the more I dug a deeper hole for myself. She felt like what we had was real—a serious relationship—like one that would soon blossom into potential marriage. Never mind the fact that I was already a married man. Karma didn't seem to acknowledge that. All she knew was that she had me, and it was all because of the sex.

It shouldn't have been hard for me to control myself, but she was an enticement or better yet a magnet. For some reason, whenever I was around her my sexual urges became insatiable. It was almost as if this lady had some type of spell on me, but I knew better. I allowed myself to be tempted the first time, and every time after that, the sex was on my brain like a drug. I continued to chase every high—every rush I'd get from doing the forbidden thing in my office.

Karma left what seemed like hundreds of messages for me over the stretch of days we were apart. Some were via voice mail, and others were sent in written form, more than likely placed into my office mailbox by a staff member. She'd seal the letters in colorful envelopes, possibly to distinguish her letters from other mail, so they wouldn't get tossed into the junk drawer in my office. I opened them and read them, but I never gave her a reply.

It was always the same ol' message with the threat of making me regret I'd been ignoring her. I wasn't going to play her game. Karma didn't want to tell on me, and I knew that. Reporting me wouldn't get her what she wanted. She'd already lost two men she thought she loved—her stepfather and Colby Patterson. She wouldn't risk losing me, too. She just wanted to irritate the hell out of me in hopes of getting a reaction or at least a response. I had no intentions of giving her what she wanted. My plan of having her ass tossed out of there was bound to work soon, and any trace of evidence of me ever being inside of her would be gone by then. I just needed to keep playing the game my way.

Work had been a little cumbersome with meetings all morning, so I finished up some paperwork and decided to head home early. I checked the remaining voice mail, deleting what was no longer needed, and leaving Karma's lengthy messages so there would only be room for a few more before the system would answer to say my voice mail was full. This way, I wouldn't have to sort through twenty more messages left by Karma.

Aisha wasn't expecting me home early. She was quite surprised when I entered through the front door. I had just checked the mailbox and didn't want to raise the garage door again. She sat up on the couch when I entered.

"You scared me," she said.

"Why? I've told you to set the alarm even when you're here."

"I thought I did," she said, lounging back on the couch.

"Baby, I know we live in a very nice neighborhood, but crime is everywhere. Please remember to set the alarm, okay?"

She nodded as she continued to stare at the TV. "You're home early."

"Um, yeah. I'm a bit tired, but I've got some work to do in my office first." I headed down the hall, and Aisha followed.

"Larry, we need to talk."

"Okay. What's up?" I walked into my office and turned on the lights.

"It's about us."

I stopped in my tracks and turned to her. "What about us? Aisha, please don't start an argument today. I'm in no mood to debate with you right now."

"I'm not trying to debate," she said with much attitude.

"Then, what's wrong? I thought we were fine."

"Larry, I just wanted to ask if we can try to get pregnant again—that's all."

I walked over to my desk and set down the folders in my hand. I couldn't believe we had to have this conversation at this moment. I'd just told her I was tired, and she saw all the proof that I'd placed on my desk. I took a seat then cupped my forehead into my hands.

"I'm lost, Aisha. What are you saying? Have we not been trying?"

"Yes—I mean, no. Remember my doctor gave us a few options for increasing our odds. I was thinking we can go ahead with the fertility treatments, and then if that doesn't work, I'm willing to try artificial insemination."

I sighed, and then looked up at her. "Aisha—"

"Wait. Before you get ready to respond, I just want you to know that I've been saving up for this. I have more than enough in my personal savings to cover this process, so you don't have to shoot me down with how much all of this will cost."

I sighed a few more times out of frustration. I pretty much gave up on us having children when I turned forty a couple of years ago. Aisha was no baby herself. At thirty-eight, she looked damned good, and I hadn't planned on changing any of that with a swollen stomach and stretch-marks. I had to say something to pacify her.

"Let me do some research on those fertility treat-ments, and I'll get back to you."

The ounce of delight she had on her face quickly dissolved. In fact, I could no longer read her expression. Her eyes were blank as she stared at me. A little uncom-fortable with the silence, I turned on my computer and began flipping through the folders. I had hoped she'd catch the hint and leave, but when she asked the next question, she had my undivided attention.

"Who's Karma Jolley?"

My eyes and my neck sprung in her direction so fast, my head started to swim with sensations of lightheaded-ness. *Speak,* I told myself. *Say something before she does.* But I couldn't. At a loss for words would be an understate-ment.

"Larry, I know you heard me. I asked a question. Who is Karma Jolley?" she repeated and took a stance that commanded an answer. Her arms were locked high at her chest and her eyebrows were raised although her eyes looked like slits.

"What? What do . . . who . . . how do you know about Karma?"

"Don't worry about all that. I just need to know why she's getting so much of the time I deserve when you're home."

I wished I could slow my heart rate. It had become difficult to speak without sounding like it wanted to jump out of my throat. I tried my best not to lead on that I was nervous, so I deepened my voice and played mad.

"Why the hell are you questioning me about one of my patients? Where did you get her name from?"

She relaxed her pose and softened her voice. "I, I, didn't know she was a patient. I was in here earlier on your computer and saw—"

"You were in my office?" Now I was mad for real. "You have a computer, an iPad, and a laptop. You have no business being in my office or on my computer."

"I know, babe, I wasn't snooping—"

"The hell you weren't! Aisha, you were looking for something that would tell you I'm cheating. Didn't I tell you we were good?"

"Yes, babe, you did. I was just messing around in here. I don't know why I came in here to be honest. I'm sorry. It's just that when I saw all the blog sites you had pulled up with her aliases, and then I saw the email you left up from the Internet detective, stating that indeed those screen names belonged to Karma Jolley—"

"You had no right, Aisha!" I slammed my fist on the desk. I stood and ripped into her feelings. "Now I'm fucking pissed! Damnit, my work is confidential, and there is no reason why I should come home and learn that my insecure ass wife has compromised my integrity as a psychiatrist."

"But I didn't learn anything personal. I just read one of her blogs about what peace means to her."

"And you don't think that's personal?"

"It's a blog—out there for the whole world to see, for goodness sakes!" she yelled right back at me.

"Get out!" I screamed, pointing to the door. "And don't you ever step foot back into this office unless I tell you."

She seemed taken aback by that demand. I knew that house was just as much hers as it was mine, but she'd crossed the lines when she dabbled on my computer. I stared her down, heaving until she did an about face and marched out the door.

I plopped down in my seat and began combing everything I left up on my computer for her to see. I spotted the email and minimized it. That's when my eyes nearly popped out of my head. Once I minimized the opened email from the detective, my inbox displayed five unread messages from Karma Jolley. *Did Aisha see these? She couldn't have.* I glanced at the times they were sent. All of them were sent between one and two o'clock—her time in the computer room. That was only an hour before I made it home.

I didn't know what to do or think because Aisha didn't say what time she'd been in my office. Surely if she had seen emails from Karma Jolley sent to my Gmail account with the subject line reading, THIS IS YOUR LAST WARNING, MY LOVE, she would have been far more upset than she was—not to mention she would have opened every message.

I opened one of the messages, and it said exactly what I thought it would—that I would soon be sorry. I warned Karma several weeks before about threatening me, but since I knew she was bluffing, I wasn't under added pressure to respond.

I tried to do some work for a while, but I didn't get much done. My mind was too consumed with thoughts of whether Aisha had seen the unread emails from Karma and how I had treated her. I didn't feel good about how I spoke to her. I was angry, and she had to feel the heat of it. I needed her to understand how much of a violation it was to go through things in my office. I always respected Aisha's privacy—never went through her purse, car, closet or anything else that she'd consider personal without her permission. I expected the same respect.

I logged off the computer after only an hour of work. I needed to go find my wife and make up with her. I didn't like going to bed angry and neither did she. We still had a few hours left before bedtime, but now was just as good of a time to make up as any.

I found Aisha in bed, under the covers, sobbing. I sat on her side of the bed next to her and pulled her to me. She had taken off her clothes, down to her bra and panties. She was a little stiff at first—reluctant to let me hold her, but only a minute later, she melted in my arms. I rocked her lightly as I shushed her.

"Baby, you know I don't like to make you cry."

"I can't help the way I feel, Larry," she said through tears into my shirt. "You treated me as though I was a child."

"I was angry, Aisha. I know I didn't come off as best as I could have. I blew up because I never thought you'd do something like that."

She pushed away from me. "I know I was wrong, and I apologized. But I wish you didn't talk to me like I was your child. You don't have kids, remember?"

"C'mere, baby," I said, reaching for her. She stiffened again. "Stop it, Aisha. C'mere." I managed to pull her to me and held her close. "I know you're not my kid, okay? So, let's say we look into having some children, and that way I'll have somebody to fuss at when I get ready."

Though it was a feeble attempt at a joke and an announcement at the same time that would make her smile, it worked. She laughed as she wiped her tears.

"You're laughing. I take it that'll be alright with you," I said, kissing her forehead. She laughed some more. "Huh? You wanna have me some kids so I can fuss at them and leave you alone?"

She raised her chin and looked into my eyes. "I would love to have your children, Dr. Weisman."

"Cool. That's what's up!" I lay her on the bed then climbed on top of her. "Then I say let's get this party started right!"

She giggled as I kissed her repeatedly all over her neck. When I stuck my tongue into her mouth, she blew out what seemed like a sigh of relief through her nose. This woman loved me, and I loved her, too. I needed to find more ways to remind her.

Aisha and I were spent after about an hour of love-making. We lay in bed discussing what we wanted to do for dinner when my cell rang. I answered it, thinking it was a call from the staff at True Hope about something I left undone. It was the staff alright, and they had far worse news. I was told I needed to return to the hospital because Karma had made a suicide attempt.

Karma

10

Sixteen freaking sleeping pills and Doc still hadn't shown up! I started collecting the pills every night once I realized Doc was playing games about seeing me again. The nurses were supposed to inspect my mouth after I swallowed the pill, but they did a half-ass job. The first night, I kept the pill under my tongue then moved it to the top of my mouth when the nurse asked to see under my tongue. That was too easy, so I decided to stash each pill until I would be ready to call Doc's bluff.

It was a risky move, taking all those pills at once, but hell I knew I wouldn't die. I made sure my new homie, Tee, would be around when I did it, so she could alert someone. Thank goodness she had some sense at that hour. I knew that if she didn't have the sense to get help, then perhaps her so-called friend, Fee-Fee would tell her what to do. But Tee was smarter than I'd given her credit for.

"Ooooo, what are you doing?" she had asked while we sat on the bench in the lawn.

"Minding my business," I answered, gulping two and three pills at a time.

"What are those?" Tee's eyes opened wide enough to see all of the white.

"Sleeping pills."

"You're not supposed to be taking meds unsupervised!" She looked as though she wanted to run. "And heeeeyyyy! You're taking way too many!"

"Leave me alone, Tee. I want to die," I lied.

Tee jumped up and ran in circles. By that time, I was done swallowing all of the pills. I sat there motionless, waiting for something inside me to happen.

"Heeeeeyyyy," Tee screamed. "Somebody quick! Get over here quick! She just took an overdose!"

And that was the start of all the chaos to get me to either throw up the pills or have my stomach pumped. Medics were called, and no matter how I tried, I couldn't throw them up. I was sick of people putting their fingers and other things into my mouth, so I started biting them.

"Karma, stop it!" a nurse screamed. "Stop biting us. Let us help you."

True Hope Psychiatric deemed me crazy, so I had to show them crazy. I cut up worse. I kicked, fought, screamed, and did more biting. Security was called to help hog-tie me, and then a decision was made to have my stomach pumped.

I was rushed into an ambulance to an emergency room, lying on my side with my hands and feet both tied behind my back. An EMT had to hold me to the stretcher. The ride was not only bumpy, but I began to feel weird. I couldn't tell if it was the pills or motion sickness. It could've been a little bit of both. Sweat consumed my body, and the stomach pains became unbearable. I screamed to the top of my lungs, and in between screams, I choked on something that threatened to erupt.

The EMTs fought hard to keep me breathing as I coughed and hacked repeatedly. I began to wonder if I'd really die. Thoughts of actually dying made me panic, increasing my heart rate and causing me to gasp for all the air I could muster.

Once we made it to the hospital, and I was rolled in on the stretcher, I felt a hint of relief. That is, until the doctor came at me with that tube to put down my throat. *Aren't they going to sedate me?* I thought. When he asked me to open my mouth, I clenched my teeth and shook my head. There was no way I would let them do that to me while I was alert. And so, there was another struggle because in between coughs and yells, the doctors fought hard to place the tube in my mouth and down my throat. *This is cruel and inhumane,* I thought.

"Sedate her," I finally heard one of the doctors say.

I was relieved. The fight was over, and I actually wanted them to hurry and get everything over with. I began to mentally beat myself up for taking those pills— and all over getting a man's attention.

When Doc didn't show up to the hospital after I requested him, I was pissed. Not only did my ploy to get his attention not seem to work, but I was transported back to True Hope immediately following the stomach pumping. That's when I refused to adhere to their demands—not until I could get what I wanted.

"NOOOOOOOOOO!" I yelled as we entered the lobby of True Hope. "I won't goooooooo! Get me Dr. Weisman nooooooowwwww!"

"Karma, get up from this floor!" a nurse fussed. "Dr. Weisman is off duty. You'll have to wait until he's in his office tomorrow."

"NOOOOOOOOO! I said noooooooowwww!"

The scene went on like that for more than likely an hour. The nurses couldn't do anything with me, and even when security tried to manhandle me, I gave them a run for their money. They picked me up and got me close to my room, but I fought even as I was being carried by two male guards—so much so that they had to put me down for a rest.

"Karma, it makes no sense for you to act like this," a nurse stated.

"SHUT THE FUCK UP! I don't want to talk to you! I want to talk to Dr. Weisman! NOOOOOWWW!" I screamed, pointing my finger in her face.

My train of thought was broken when I saw two male nurses rushing up behind her to get at me. One carried a straight jacket. Security grabbed me from behind, and then I crouched to the floor, kicking and screaming. My arms were stretched in many uncomfortable directions, but that didn't stop me from fighting. However, they still managed to restrain me.

They might have won the battle, but the war wasn't over. What they didn't know was that I still had fight in me. When I could no longer use my hands due to the jacket, I used my mouth as a weapon and tossed spit to and fro. Everyone's faces went from concerned to anger. I spit in a security officer's face, and then kicked him in the knee. He gripped his knee and gave me the evil eye as my saliva ran down the side of his face. The entire staff grew very tired of me.

"That's it," a nurse yelled, her voice stern and affirming. "Get a needle! We're going to sedate her."

"But Dr. Weisman hasn't called back and given us that order," a male nurse said.

"Damn, that! We have no choice when she's irrepressible," she responded in her authoritative voice.

The male nurse nodded then jumped up, scurrying from the scene, but he didn't get far before he was stopped by a firm, masculine voice that commanded, "That won't be necessary!"

Everyone's attention was drawn to Dr. Weisman. Though he had a look of contempt toward me, I felt a sense of relief. I could take it easy, and hell, I was tired. It wasn't easy maintaining such chaotic energy at that level for an hour. Doc stepped into the madness large and in charge.

"Get her out of that restraint," he demanded.

"Dr. Weisman, I don't think we should do that. She's been—" the female nurse started.

"I said get her out!"

I was quite proud of Doc. He had stepped into his superior role, and it was very attractive. A grin trembled at the corners of my lips, threatening to expose my inner thoughts, but I managed to keep a straight face. The security men assisted the male nurse with standing me up, so they could release the straight jacket. Doc came within inches of my face, killing what little glee I had begun to feel.

"Listen to me. Once they get that jacket off you, you are *not* to act a fool in any way," he said through clenched teeth. "You *will* behave yourself. Or, I will have you tossed out of here and on your way to prison tonight! Do I make myself clear?"

When I didn't answer, he placed his hand on the male nurse's arm, stopping him from unfastening the straight jacket.

He repeated himself. "Do I make myself clear?"

I squinted in anger and answered, "Abundantly."

Doc released the man's arm before continuing his disdain for me.

"I, nor my staff, appreciate having to deal with your unruly behavior at any time—let alone so late in the evening." I rolled my eyes and glared at the ceiling as he continued. "You are not the only patient we have to tend to, but you *are* the only one we repeatedly have issues with. Your behavior is unacceptable, and we will not tolerate it anymore."

I lowered my chin so that my eyes could meet his. "We need to talk," I simply said.

"You're going to politely allow this staff to walk you to your room, and I don't want to hear another word."

That's when Doc's colleague and friend, Dr. Steven M. Johnson, showed up. "Everything all right, Dr. Weisman?"

Dr. Johnson's visit was not coincidental. I knew that because he and Doc had been off duty for hours. Plus, the fact that Dr. Johnson had on jeans, tennis shoes and a University of Memphis T-shirt instead of his normal slacks, dress shirt and tie let me know that Doc had called him from home to his rescue. My blood began to percolate. If Doc thought inviting his friend into the situation would hinder our meeting, he had another guess coming. He turned to his friend.

"Yes, Dr. Johnson, everything is fine," he answered, keeping his eyes on me. "I was just explaining to Karma that she will behave herself from now on. She was just about to retire to her room."

"The hell I am!" I yelled. "I said we need to talk. NOW!"

Doc knew I wasn't backing down. His face went from confident to concerned in a matter of seconds as he took notice of my chest heaving after losing most of my wind from screaming at him. Dr. Johnson tried to soothe the situation with his smooth-talking ass.

"Now, Karma, you know all that screaming is uncalled for." Dr. Johnson's voice was low and amiable. "C'mon, girl, let's call it a night and have this discussion in the morning."

He reached out and placed a friendly hand on my shoulder. I glanced at the ashy folds between the sockets of his fingers and the raggedy beds of his fingernails and wondered what the hell else he did for a living besides being a psychiatrist. I caught him off guard when I slapped his hand off my shoulder, causing him to jump.

"Karma!" Dr. Johnson yelled, forgetting all about his once receptive tone. "We're all trying to be nice here!"

"I wasn't talking to you, motherfucker! My business is with him," I said, pointing to Doc.

"C'mon, Dr. Johnson," Doc said. "Let's meet with her in my office."

"Oh, no! Not him. Just me and you."

"Karma, there will be no meeting if Dr. Johnson can't sit in on it."

"Okay, then let's all pull up some chairs right here. If he gets to be a fly on the wall, then all of these mutherfuckers can be in on our conversation." The stunned faces around me seemed not to know what to do or say. "Or, shall I just start since it seems you don't need a seat?"

Doc sighed heavily then brushed his hand over the top of his head a few times. Dr. Johnson seemed at a loss for words, too. He glanced back and forth between Doc and me many times, shaking his head. Doc gave me his reluctant answer.

"I have five minutes I can spare, and that's all," he said.

"You'll only need two," I snapped.

Doc beckoned security to follow us down the hall, which was routine, but Dr. Johnson's presence was what irritated me most. He stood outside the office with security, and for what, I didn't know. Doc demanded answers shortly after closing the door.

"What the hell are you doing, Karma? Why the fuck did you take those pills?"

"I was missing you."

My calmness should've been enough to keep the conversation at a peaceful level, but Doc didn't seem to get the hint as he yelled at me some more.

"Missing me? Missing me? You were fucking missing me, so you go and swallow enough pills to kill your damned self?"

"C'mon, Doc, you know I had no intentions of dying. I just wanted what we have right now," I said, stepping closer to him. "Some solitude—quality time together, you know." I slid my hands up his chest, tracing his nipples through his all-black T-shirt.

He grabbed my wrists. "Do you really think I'm going to fuck you with those people so close outside my door? Security may not suspect anything, but Dr. Johnson will."

"Sssshhh," I whispered as I rested my head on his chest. "We can be extremely quiet."

I took a long whiff of him, and then jumped back, disgusted. I was enraged all over again. He looked confused.

"What's wrong?"

He got the answer when I drew back and slapped him with so much force, it made him stumble.

"How *dare* you come to see me smelling like sex and perfume!"

He was clearly dazed as he stood rubbing the side of his face. That meeting was over. I was so mad, I couldn't stomach the site of him. I barged out of his office and headed straight to my room, ignoring the fact that security really should have been escorting me. They weren't far behind though as they trotted to catch up with me. I fussed under my breath all the way to my room and slammed the door.

I passed dumbfounded nurses along the way. I'm sure they didn't know what to think. I wasn't even sure what to think, but I did know Doc hadn't heard the last of me. He could send me to prison if he wanted, but I would make him regret the day he ever crossed me first.

Lawrence

11

*O*ne week after the stunt Karma pulled with swallowing those pills, things still hadn't gotten better for me. Aisha began to receive more calls—not just to the house but to her cell phone as well. I had given permission to the staff to let Karma have more time in the computer room, and I even relaxed the rules so she could take her aggression out in her blogs. My hope was that if she was preoccupied on the computer, she'd be less focused on the fact that she couldn't see me.

As the days seemed to fly by without a response from my request to transfer Karma, I suffered tremendously with stress. I just wanted Karma out of my hair before she got some bright idea or notion that she should just go ahead and destroy my career. My marriage was already in trouble. Aisha had begun to think the calls were definitely from someone I was sleeping with. I couldn't convince her otherwise. She'd also stopped having sex with me.

I sat at my desk, thinking about how I had just wanted my wife to do anything to please me before I had to be at work, but she simply refused. I rubbed between her legs, but she fought, argued and pushed me away. Her change in attitude was all my fault, and at the same time it wasn't. Karma was just evil. I could only hope that after I got Karma out of the way, she'd find another distraction at her new facility and leave me and my wife alone.

My office phone startled me as it rang. I glanced at the caller ID and realized it could be the call I'd been hoping to receive.

"True Hope—Dr. Weisman speaking. How may I help you?"

"Dr. Weisman, this is Rhoda King from the administrative office in admissions."

"Ok, great. How are you today, Ms. King?"

"I'm wonderful. How are you?"

"Ready for a vacation, but other than that I'll live," I answered, light-heartedly.

"I think we all could use a good vacation," she said as she chuckled.

"So, what can I do for you, Ms. King?"

I sat at my desk, listening intently as the caller did not bare the news I wanted to hear. Instead, I was told that my petition to have Karma transferred, first to another doctor, and then to another hospital was denied due to failure to report sufficient reasons True Hope could no longer adequately treat her at our facility.

"So, tell me, Ms. King: How do I fix this? Or, at least how do I get the first request of her being treated by Dr. Steven M. Johnson approved?"

"Well, Dr. Weisman, since you clearly disagree with this decision, you could rewrite the petition and resubmit it at any time. I can't guarantee anything favorable, but if nothing else, perhaps your first request will be approved with sufficient reasoning since Ms. Jolley will still be housed in True Hope."

"And what if my petition is rejected again?"

"It won't be as long as you make certain to write the key factors that were missing in the first petition."

I sighed. "And I suppose several more weeks will go by before I'll receive an answer, right?"

"Yes, it does take time, Dr. Weisman. Oh, and keep in mind that once it has been reviewed and accepted, then a court date could be set to determine the patient's outcome."

I pretended to be all right with what I'd learned. "That'll be great, Ms. King. I thank you for getting back to me as soon as you could."

"No problem, Dr. Weisman. Just give me a heads up when you plan to resubmit the petition. I'll keep an eye out for it."

"I will, and thanks again."

I hung up and crashed my upper body on top of my desk. I was bombed. Karma would never act right in a court room if it came to that. She'd do everything possible to make me look bad. I just wanted her transferred without her ever knowing what happened. I couldn't wait to end that call. My head rested on my forearms on my desk. I didn't get up until I heard two light taps and then the door opened.

"What's up, Doc? Can we have a meeting?" Steve teased in his Karma voice.

I shook my head. "Man, I'm in no mood to play."

"Uh-oh. What's wrong now?" Steve quickly closed the door.

I stood and walked around to lean on the front of my desk. "I'm sick of the bullshit, that's all!"

"Um, you mind telling me what bullshit that would be?"

"The bullshit dealing with Karma."

"Oh, hell, I should've guessed. I thought you were talking about something new. What has she done now?"

"Nothing yet, but I just got that call I've been wanting since what seems like forever now."

"And? What's the word?" Steve sat in the seat in front of my desk.

"It wasn't anything good."

"What? Why not?"

"The damn petition was denied."

"Oh, c'mon! You've got to be kidding me. What were the reasons?"

"Insufficient notes detailing reasoning for her transfer to another doctor, and why our facility can no longer provide adequate treatment to her."

"Oh, snap. Didn't see that one coming."

"Hell, neither did I? I've never had to remove a patient from my care."

"Okay, so now what?"

"Well, I was thinking that I could just rewrite the petition, stating my patient list is too full, hence needing to transfer her to someone . . . yada, yada, yada."

"'Yada, yada' my ass! I mean, we can't have her transferred into my care without a plan 'B'. And don't you even think of it! You're not gonna leave me stuck with her ass, if they approve the next petition for doctor transfer."

"Yeah, and as I lay sulking on my desk, I was thinking plan 'B' has to be to expedite her ass to prison. That'll be the easiest thing to do."

Steve nodded slowly. He looked as if wheels were spinning in his head. "True . . . true. I mean, she has caused a lot of trouble here."

"Well, not just that, but I'm thinking I may just have to schedule more frequent meetings so I can gradually declare her sane in the notes."

"Very nice plan, but man, let me tell you something. You've gotta stop having sex with that girl."

"I know, I know, and I'm done."

"No, seriously, Lawrence. You say that, and then when she's around you, you can't seem to keep your dick in your pants."

"I totally hear you. And I'm telling you I'm done."

"Be honest. You got some kind of sex addiction or something?"

I shook my head. "Naw, that couldn't be it. I mean, it's just something about Karma. She's got some kind of who-doo or something that she does to people, I guess. Hey, I'm not the only man she was able to seduce, you know."

"Yeah, and where are all the others? Dead?"

"Not all of 'em."

Steve gave me an incredulous smirk, and then we both found a laugh in what I'd just said.

"Well, hell, I ain't dead," I said matter-of-factly.

"Not yet. I'm telling you: Keep your dick in your pants. I don't wanna be reading about what a great man you were in your obituary."

I shook my head. "Naw, naw. Believe me, man. I'm done."

"A'ight, so how soon do you think it would be before you'd have enough to type up from your sessions, so her ass can be gone?"

"Maybe three months—you know, just to make it look good. Besides, my past files never stated she was insane. I only said just enough to keep her here."

"Cool. Sounds like you have a plan then."

"Man, I'm keeping my fingers crossed."

We heard two more taps on the door, and then turned in its direction when the door swung open.

"Oh, I'm sorry," Nurse Mitchell said. "I didn't know you had someone in here. I can come back." She started backing out of the office.

"Um, is there something I can help you with, Nurse Mitchell?" I asked just before she closed the door.

"Pardon?" She reentered the office.

"Did you need to speak with me?" I asked.

"Yes, Dr. Weisman, if you don't mind—it's about a patient."

Steve jumped up as if that was his cue to leave. He spoke to her on his way out.

"Been doing all right, Ms. Mitchell?" he asked.

"Yes, Dr. Johnson, I'm doing very well. Thanks for asking."

"Good . . . good," he responded then turned his attention to me. "Dr. Weisman, I think you've got it all figured out now, and if you need to run something else by me, I'll be in my office."

"Thanks, Dr. Johnson. Have a good one."

Steve nodded at both of us and then exited my office. I gestured for Nurse Mitchell to have a seat. She walked over to the seat Steve once sat in and eased into it. She was eerily quiet for someone who said she wanted to speak with me, so I broke the ice.

"Is everything all right, Nurse Mitchell?"

"Um, not really."

"Oh?"

"Well, I wanted to first let you know that Karma has been requesting to see you."

"I told you—"

"I know you specifically requested that I not place her on your schedule for now, but she isn't taking no for an answer."

"Well, she doesn't have very much of a choice, does she, Nurse Mitchell?"

Until then, she'd been glancing all around the room as she spoke to me. This time she glared straight into my eyes.

"Are you screwing her, Dr. Weisman?"

I was blown away by her gall. "What?" I snapped.

"You heard me," she responded, not backing down. "Are you having sex with your mentally ill patient?"

"Well, Nurse Mitchell, that would be inappropriate, immoral, and unethical."

"It would also be grounds for termination and a law suit, possibly criminal, if you're found to have taken advantage of her."

I shifted my weight and crossed my arms as I continued to lean on my desk. *The nerve of this bitch!* I thought as I stared at her unblinkingly. I knew exactly what this was about.

"What do you want from me, Darla? Huh? Are you mad because I ended our very brief affair?"

"Hell yeah I'm mad. But not for the reasons you think I am. I don't want your dick. I can get that from anywhere. I'm mad because you used me."

"Darla, nobody used you," I said, heading to sit at my desk. "I've got marvelous pussy at home. I didn't need to have sex with you."

"Then you should've kept your dick restricted to her pasty whole," she quipped. She pointed as she spoke. "You used me to get my staff to vote you for the hospital's True Hope Choice Award, not only ensuring you another six years under contract here, but also a hefty sixty thousand dollar bonus."

I chuckled, a bit amazed that she would insinuate that I needed her. What she didn't take into consideration was the level of hard work and commitment I'd put into the hospital before that award was even in the making. The staff's vote was only ten percent of how the award was decided. I would have won with or without her staff. My work spoke for itself, and she wasn't as clueless as she sat in my office portraying to be.

"The proof is in the doing—check my records. I worked my ass off, not only with patients, but with getting charitable contributions and personally funding research as needed. And just so you know, I'm well-paid. So as for the bonus, it measures up to a measly ten thousand dollars extra per year. I could never let that make *or* break me."

She smirked. "Hmph," was all she said.

"You know all of that, Darla, but then again I guess since you came in here with an ulterior motive, recognizing my accomplishments would be the last thing you want to establish. So, let me ask you again: What do you want from me?"

She slid to the edge of her seat. "I want you to stop fucking her. She's still a kid compared to you and me, and she needs real psychiatric help."

Now we were getting to the bottom of her feelings, but I would never lead on that she was right about Karma and me. I pretended to be confused.

"Well, see, now that's where I'm going to have to ask you to leave. You insist on accusing me of being a man without integrity—"

"You're screwing her," she said, interrupting me. "I can't prove it, but I know you are. You manipulated me. I thought we could have something, until you finally wore your wedding ring, that is."

"Excuse me? Oh, I ended the affair, remember?"

"Not until I questioned your ring. Contrary to what you write, Lawrence, the girl is ill. She's been hurt enough. She doesn't deserve your abuse. If you leave her alone, I won't report you, and you can continue to work here as long as you agree to tweak your schedule to an all-male patient list."

I went over and lifted Darla's arm to help her out of the seat. "This chat has been enlightening, Nurse Mitchell, but I do have things to do. We will have to pick up this conversation at a later date. Hopefully by then you will be both well-informed and apologetic for your behavior today." I walked her over to the door, opened it, and lightly shoved her on the other side of it. "You have a great day now. Buh-bye."

The door closed just a little harder than I had intended. I didn't want Darla to know she had gotten to me. She blindsided me. I had no idea she even thought I could possibly be sleeping with Karma. And if she thought it, who else thought it? The whole situation with Karma would be magnified with Darla on her team.

Darla had been bitter for five years, barely speaking to me, and it was all over me deciding not to keep seeing her. We had sex once, and then I realized I made a mistake. I didn't want to have an affair. Sex with Darla was just something that just kind of happened after a little play talk that she started. I felt obligated to take her out a time or two after sleeping with her in my office, but my conscience wouldn't let me keep seeing her. So, I ended it.

I sat at my desk, realizing I was in real trouble. I could kiss my career and wife goodbye, if I didn't get my dilemma fixed soon.

Karma

12

---

*T*uesday again—time to play catch up with WhiteKnight. Doc not only lifted my restrictions, but he also upgraded the number of days I could go to the computer room. I could now get online three days a week—Tuesday, Thursdays, and Fridays. I didn't utilize all the days each week, but it was good knowing the option was there, if need be.

WhiteKnight had me curious to know more about him every time we chatted. We'd gotten closer as Internet buddies lately. I learned that his real name was Wayne. He didn't look like a Wayne to me, but maybe he did to his mother. I didn't ask. I just said okay to the name. I told him my first name, too. He thought my name was beautiful and exceptional. No one had ever told me that before. This guy was pretty unique and in a different class himself.

Wayne actually seemed like a pretty nice guy. He always asked about my feelings. I never told him the truth though. I didn't want to scare him off by telling him I was in a mental hospital. I just gave him white lies like I was living with relatives and couldn't have visitors. I also told him I was an evaluator for a research company. I figured he must've believed it because he didn't bother questioning me on what exactly I did as an evaluator.

He still wouldn't let me in on what he did for a living. He must've known I was smarter than the average gal because as soon as he would give me his business name, I was going to do some investigating.

When I stepped into the computer room, I noticed I had free pick of any of the seats in the room. Either no one else wanted to get online at that hour or they were all on restrictions. That didn't matter to me. The privacy would do me some good, I was sure.

Shortly after the ol' library Grinch closed the door to the computer room, I logged on to my eLovers Row account and looked for WhiteKnight. He was there. Just as I knew he'd be. I hurriedly typed him a message.

HEY WHY IS IT EVERY TIME I LOG ON, YOU'RE HERE?

I patiently waited for his response. He was usually pretty quick about responding to me. This time around was no different.

WHY DO YOU THINK? he typed back.
'CAUSE YOU'RE BUSY FLIRTING WITH OTHER WOMEN.
IS THAT WHAT YOU THINK?
YOU BETTER NOT BE.
I ASKED IF THAT'S WHAT YOU THINK.

PERHAPS.

WOW. I SEE WE STILL HAVE SOME GROWING TO DO.

I wasn't sure what he meant by that, and it kind of hurt my feelings. It sounded as if he called me immature. I had to get to the bottom of that comment.

HMM. I'M HURT, I told him.

WHY?

I THINK YOU'RE SAYING I'M NOT MATURE.

LOL NOT WHAT I'M SAYING AT ALL.

THEN WHAT ARE YOU SAYING?

I MEANT WE STILL DON'T KNOW EACH OTHER WELL ENOUGH. I THOUGHT YOU'D THINK BETTER OF ME THAN TO BE FLIRTING WITH OTHER WOMEN.

BUT YOU'RE ALWAYS ONLINE.

IT JUST SEEMS THAT WAY.

SO YOU'RE NOT CHATTING WITH OTHER WOMEN?

I'M NOT.

THEN HOW IS IT YOU'RE ONLINE WHEN I GET ON?

BECAUSE I'VE FIGURED OUT YOUR ROUTINE.

I'M THAT PREDICTABLE?

YOU ARE.

WOW. THEN I GUESS I OWE YOU AN APOLOGY.

NO APOLOGY NEEDED.

THANKS ☺

SO HOW MUCH TIME CAN YOU SPARE ME TODAY?

HOW MUCH TIME DO YOU NEED? I enjoyed flirting with him. He was a breath of fresh air.

I KNOW YOU'RE A BUSY WOMAN, SO I'LL TAKE WHATEVER
I CAN GET.

I SEE WE'RE GOING TO GET ALONG VERY WELL, WAYNE.

I FIGURED THAT A LONG TIME AGO.

HOW?

I LOVE THE WAY I FEEL WHEN I CHAT WITH YOU.

ARE YOU FALLING IN LOVE?

I THINK SO.

I was stunned at his response to say the least. I only threw that question out there, halfway joking. I didn't expect the answer he gave me. The chat became even more interesting for me.

HMM. AND YOU HAVEN'T EVEN SEEN ME YET, I told him.

IT DOESN'T MATTER. I KNOW YOU'RE BEAUTIFUL.

HOW DO YOU KNOW?

I JUST KNOW.

LET'S MEET. I RATHER YOU SEE ME IN PERSON.

I'M IN LONDON.

I KNOW. BUT WE CAN PLAN TO MEET SOON.

YOU'RE RIGHT. I PROMISED YOU A TRIP HERE, DIDN'T I?

AND I'M HOLDING YOU TO IT.

OK. LET ME CLEAR SOME THINGS ON MY SCHEDULE FIRST
AND GET BACK TO YOU.

I'M EXCITED.

GLAD TO HEAR THAT, MY DEAR.

WILL YOU GIVE ME A PERSONAL TOUR?

FOR SURE. I CAN'T WAIT.

I HOPE YOU MEAN THAT.

I DO.

I was so wrapped up into my chat that I didn't hear or see the librarian come in. She startled me as I sat reading Wayne's last response.

"Will you be checking out books today, Karma?"

I jumped then held my chest. "Huh? What? You scared me?"

She twisted her mouth as she always did then said, "Well, if you weren't doing something you don't have no business, you wouldn't be so startled."

"I beg your pardon. I'm not under restrictions anymore. Dr. Weisman said I could visit any site I wanted to."

"Yes, as long as it's within guidelines, and as long as you don't find one of those porn sites True Hope hasn't been able to restrict yet. You know new ones keep popping up every day."

"Do I look like I would be on a porn site?"

"I don't know what you look like," she snapped. "I really don't look atcha that hard. But you better not be on any sites dealing with drugs, alcohol or firearms either."

I shook my head then twisted my mouth at her. Just then another response popped up from Wayne.

BY THE WAY, YOU NEVER TOLD ME WHEN I'D GET THAT PRETTY PICTURE OF YOU.

The librarian must've read it at the same time I did. "You better not be uploading pictures to nobody online."

I minimized the screen. "C'mon now. How would I do that? I don't have access to pictures of me."

"I'm just saying. You better not. If Dr. Weisman knew this is what you're doing with your time in here, he'd put you on restrictions again."

"What am I doing? I'm having an innocent conversation with a friend. Go. Leave me alone. I don't want no books or nothing else from you. Just please . . . can you please leave me alone?"

"I'ma leave you alone alright. Don't make me go and tell Dr. Weisman he needs to come in here."

I sighed heavily. This woman was a thorn in my side. I was trying to enjoy my hour in the computer room, and not think about the fact that Doc had totally pissed me off last time I saw him, but Library Grinch refused to let me do so.

"Go," I screamed at her. "Go tell him. Go tell him whatever you want! Just leave me the hell alone."

She rolled her eyes at me. "Hmph," she said just before storming off, closing the door behind her.

It felt good to be alone again. At some point while I was yelling at the librarian, Wayne must've sent another message because I saw one I hadn't read.

HELLO? KARMA, WHERE ARE YOU?

I'M SORRY, WAYNE. I HAD TO ANSWER THE DOOR REAL QUICK.

YOU'VE GOT COMPANY?

NOT ANYMORE.

SO I HAVE YOUR UNDIVIDED ATTENTION.

I'M ALL YOURS.

We engaged in more satisfying small talk for long while. I began to think that if this guy was in the states, he very well could've made me forget all about the fact that I loved Doc. Time seemed to fly just because I was having fun. I had roughly another ten minutes to spare in the computer room.

OK. SO ABOUT THAT PICTURE OF YOU, he asked.

I'M SORRY, BABE, BUT THIS OL' RAGGEDY COMPUTER WOULDN'T LET ME UPLOAD ONE. I TRIED JUST A MINUTE AGO.

NOW THAT MAKES ME SAD. ☹

DON'T BE. I'LL FIGURE OUT A WAY TO GET ONE TO YOU. NO PROBLEM.

GOOD.

SO TELL ME WHY SOME LUCKY MAN HASN'T SNATCHED YOU UP YET.

ALL MY EXES WERE JERKS.

REALLY?

YES. I CAN'T MENTION ANY NAMES BECAUSE WITH YOUR WEALTH AND PRESTIGE, YOU JUST MIGHT KNOW THEM.

I DOUBT IT. I DON'T KNOW MANY AMERICANS.

WELL LET'S JUST SAY THE LATEST ONE'S LAST NAME IS WEISMAN, AND I'M REALLY PISSED AT HIM.

I waited for Wayne to ask me why, but he didn't respond. After about a minute of no reply, I posted another comment.

WAYNE? ARE YOU THERE?

Still no reply. I looked at the time and noticed I only had a few minutes left.

WAYNE? WHERE ARE YOU? I HAVE TO LEAVE IN A FEW MINUTES.

C'mon, c'mon, c'mon, I thought as I tapped my fingernails on the table. This was unlike Wayne. He usually had to wait around for me. When the door swung open, I expected the librarian to walk in, but she didn't. The stature in the door way caught me completely off guard.

"Karma, let's go to my office. We need to talk."

Doc looked as though he was partially out of breath, which made me nervous because I couldn't imagine what might've happened. He obviously had some bad news for me or else he wouldn't have barged in the way he did. I didn't know what to say to Doc, so I said nothing. I just typed a quick goodbye to Wayne then logged off.

Ms. Grinch finally showed up, standing behind Doc, pretending to be innocent.

"What'd she do?" she asked. "What did she do, Dr. Weisman?"

Doc just shook his head and walked off. I followed along side security as Doc headed toward the other side of the building. *Don't start no shit, won't be no shit,* is what came to my mind as I stared at the back of Doc's head. I was sure this meeting would prove to be interesting, and I couldn't wait.

Lawrence

13

---

*K*arma seemed elated to be seated across from me at my desk. We stared at each other for a couple of minutes. She seemed to be collecting her thoughts just as much as I was, but with her, who could really tell? I couldn't imagine she had a clue why I'd called her into my office. I was still a bit uncertain I should even have her in there with me, but what I had to say couldn't wait. It was time to get back into her good graces and make her trust me again.

She sat, seemingly absorbing an eyeful of me. Perhaps it was because she couldn't be sure when she'd be able to see me again. I sat up and stared straight into her eyes to see if I could get to the core of her thoughts.

"How've you been, Karma?"

"I'm good, Doc, and you?"

"I'm great. Thanks for asking—"

"Are we about to start a session or something?" Her voice was high-pitched and anxious.

The curiosity I'd seen in her eyes seemed to have gotten the best of her. I could tell as she sat rocking her crossed leg back and forth at the knee that she was restless and wanted me to get to the point of our meeting. But she caught me off guard. I was supposed to lead the discussion. She was being Karma though. I shouldn't have expected anything different. I stared at her, sort of in a daze, but she snapped me back.

"Doc? What's up? Is this a session? Are you about to evaluate me?" She planted both feet flat on the floor, and her upper body was erect like a meerkat.

"Huh? Session? Um, no," I stammered. "I thought I'd just bring you in here for a brief moment since we hadn't spoken in a while—to make sure you're doing okay since our last encounter," I lied.

"You mean since I had to slap the shit out of you?" she quipped, rolling her neck.

I cleared my throat and loosened my tie. "Um, yes—that day. How have things been with you?"

"I told you I'm good."

She sat back and crossed her legs. Had she known she'd be seeing me, she might've worn a skirt for my viewing pleasure like in the past. I'm glad I caught her off guard. As far as I was concerned, we would never fool around sexually again, but I was careful not to throw mixed signals at her.

"Good . . . good . . . I'm glad to hear that. You know Karma, I'm going to start our sessions again real soon. I'm working on my upcoming calendar as we speak."

I could've sworn I saw sparkles in her eyes. "When? I'm ready. Are you ready?"

"Well, yeah, if you're talking about your sessions where I actually counsel you and take notes, then yes, I'm ready."

She seemed disappointed. "Oh," she said as she sat back. "Well, that's okay. We can do those, too."

We stared at each other for a moment. I knew her last comment meant she had hopes she'd be able to convince me to do the things with her I once did, but my intentions were far from that. I wanted nothing more sexually to do with that girl. I needed to be able to document her visits and declare her mentally sane as soon as possible. Basically, I wanted to write her out of my life as soon as the opportunity produced.

Before I could say another word, she squinted and shook her finger at me. "You know, Doc, I'm still pissed about you coming to see me just after you finished pulling your dick out of your wife."

I cleared my throat and briefly scratched my scalp — a nervous gesture, I suppose. I liked the nerve of her to tell me what not to do with my wife. Yes, I'd jumped out of bed with my wife and not showered. I also knew there was a chance Karma was either dying or critical after taking all those pills, so when I was asked to rush to the ER, I did. Whether I smelled like sweat, sex, or perfume was the farthest thing on my mind. What I wanted to hurry and find out was whether my nightmare called Karma had ended with her death.

The more I pondered what to say, the more agitated Karma seemed. "You really don't understand the love I have for you, do you?"

Karma got up and started toward me. I stood and held out a halt hand. She popped her neck and batted her eyes as if to say, "Oh, no he didn't!" But she didn't say that. She stood in place and said something far worse, instead.

"Um, nigga, puh-leeze!" She fixed her hand on her hip.

"Excuse me?"

"Um, you can put that hand down," she said as she started toward me again. "We both know the real reason you called me in here," she said, grabbing at my pants, "and I don't think we have much time before someone tries to interrupt, so let's get to it."

I grabbed at her hands and wrestled hard to keep them from my crotch.

"No, Karma, listen. Hey, I do know how much you love me." That stopped her tussle. "I do. It doesn't seem like I do, but I do, okay?"

"Then why don't you act like you know?"

"Because, Karma . . . I'm your doctor—your psychiatrist. I can't show affection toward you publicly—"

"Un-un. I'm not talking about that. I'm talking about in here. You used to show me you cared."

I stared at her because the truth couldn't possibly help her at this point. I only cared about what we did without our clothes on, but it wasn't entirely my fault. Karma was voracious. She came ready and willing every time we met. She could turn me on with her eyes and her words, let alone nudity and foreplay. Even this meeting was uncomfortable—her standing so close to me, batting her eyes and licking her lips. I needed to get myself together.

"Hey, listen, we can talk about anything you want once we begin your next session, okay?" I lied.

"Why not now? I'm in here now," she said, snatching her hands from me.

"Well, I would like to know about the overdose situation. What's up with that?"

"Hmph. I don't want to talk about that."

"So, you think you get to pick and choose what we do and talk about?"

She shrugged. "I mean, maybe we'll talk about that next time, but I'd much rather be doing other things with you right now."

"Well, we can't."

"Why?" She damned near startled me with her quick, loud tone.

"Because I have a meeting in a few," I answered, lying once again.

"Oh, yeah? Another patient?"

"No, Karma. This is a business meeting."

She rolled her eyes. "Hmph. Like I really believe that."

I had to diffuse her before she started a fire with her anger. "Karma, I care about how you feel. I do."

"You do?" she asked softly.

"Yes. That's why we need to begin your sessions again."

"Well, okay," she said, heading to take a seat. "I'll come prepared." She sat then smirked at me.

I had to loosen my tie some more. She wasn't supposed to make me so nervous, but she did. I changed the subject.

"So, Karma, how are you enjoying the new Internet privileges? Have you reconnected with friends on your blog?"

Her wandering eyes let me know she was readying her thoughts for a lie. "Mm-hmm," she forced out with a nod.

"Really? So, what are you writing about?"

"Um . . . you know . . . um—stuff."

"What kind of stuff, Karma? You don't mention me or this center do you?"

"Huh?"

"Karma, I think I need to tell you that for your own safety, you must not mention this facility or anyone in it, and that includes me. Make certain you never compromise the safety and security of yourself or anyone here. Okay?"

She nodded. "Okay."

"Good. I'm glad I remembered to share that with you. I know I've mentioned it before. I just felt the need to reiterate that."

"Oh, I'll be careful."

"Thank you. Now is there anything else we need to talk about before I dismiss this meeting?"

She shook her head. "I just want to know how long it'll be before you schedule our session."

"I can't readily say right now, but I think we can begin as early as next week."

"Next week!" she shrieked. "But it's only Tuesday. Doc, we haven't had a meeting in a long while."

"I'm well aware of that, Karma, but let me just add that once we start the new sessions, you are to practice self-control at all times."

"Practice self-control? Who do I look like to you, Doc? Huh? A five-year-old?"

"That's not what—"

She stood. "Well, I'm not! I'm a grown-ass woman, and you don't have to tell me to practice self-control."

"You didn't let me finish," I said, remaining calm. "Have a seat." Once she plopped down into the chair, crossing her arms at her chest to sulk, I finished my statement. "You are to practice self-control at all times, meaning no loud-talking or talking over me, no storming out of here because you are mad, and please . . . keep your hands, feet and objects to yourself."

She stood again and started toward the door. "I know you think I'm a fool," she said over her shoulder. "Preschoolers get told to keep their hands, feet and objects to themselves." She stopped just at the door and faced me. "I'm going back to the computer room. The next time you want to interrupt me for a visit, make sure you really want something. Otherwise, leave me the hell alone. I've got better things to do than to sit in here and let you insult me."

She stormed out of the office, leaving the door cracked. I got up to make sure security saw her and would escort her back to the computer room.

I peeped out the door and saw the officer walking closely behind her. I had to chuckle a bit. Karma was furious that I hadn't led on that she and I would begin our sessions as the usual business. Her little tantrum on the way out meant nothing to me. As far as I was concerned, the ball was back in my court, and it would stay that way—or so I thought.

Karma

14

*T*hat Lawrence Weisman would see the bad side of me yet. All I wanted him to do was stop faking—pretending as if he didn't love me. He loved me. And not only did he love me, but he loved what I could offer him between my legs— a mound of sexual heat.

I called Doc's office the next day, thinking he would at least tell me my next scheduled visitation, but instead, he gave me a bullshitting line about how his calendar hadn't been approved. I was past sick of his games. I wanted and needed that man in my life. He was the best friend I had at the time. Yeah, there was Tee and Wayne, but who could really count them. Hell, Tee was loony, and Wayne only existed on the computer. I could touch Doc, and he could touch me.

My relatives on both my parents' sides still wanted nothing to do with me. I often thought my relatives didn't want anything to do with me because perhaps they thought they'd have to help provide financial means for my mental health treatment or care for me in other ways. Or it could've been they didn't trust me after what I did to cause my parents' deaths—either way, if they didn't want me, I didn't want any of them either. I just wanted Doc.

It was Thursday, and I could go back to the computer room. I sat on the back lawn with Tee, waiting until my scheduled computer time. We played cards again. I asked Fee-Fee to go to the library and make sure nobody skipped my turn. Tee didn't seem to like me sending her "girl" away, but I wasn't in the mood for her talking to the air and shit. I hardly wanted to play cards, so she was lucky I was even doing that much. Tee slammed the ace of spades on the small patio table.

"I'm cuttin'," she said proudly.

"Cuttin' what, Tee?" I shook my head. "I haven't played anything."

"Oh, that's right." She picked up the ace. "Well, play then."

"But it's not my turn. You have to play a card and then I'll play."

She looked puzzled then reached into her hand and slammed a five of diamonds on the table. "Play up!" she demanded.

I placed a three of spades on top of her card then tried to collect the book. Tee placed her hand on top of mine, stopping me.

"Hey, no fair, Karma! That's my book."

"No, Tee, I'm cuttin' your diamond. See," I said, holding up my spade. "I don't have any diamonds."

"Karma, you really like to cheat, don't you? I think that's why you sent Fee-Fee away. You knew she'd watch my back."

"What are you talking about, Tee?"

"I'm sayin' you wouldn't let me play my spade, but then when it's your turn, you played your spade."

I could've screamed. *Why do I keep taking myself through this*, I asked myself. Tee liked playing cards, bless her heart, but she didn't know how to, and it was nerve-wracking trying to teach her. I slid the book to her.

"My bad, Tee. You're right. Let's just chat for a bit. You know, we haven't had girl chat in a while."

Tee frowned as she scooped her cards and began straightening them. She hadn't let out her annoying giggle in a while. I couldn't tell if she was mad because she thought I'd cheated or because I suggested we stop playing. My mind was elsewhere though.

"So, Tee, I was thinking: Why don't we set something up so I can spend a few hours away from here. I'm curious to see if we could really pull this off."

"Well, first, I'll have to ask my sister if she would be willing to do it."

"Tell her your friend is lonely and has no family or friends on the outside, and that I just want to be able to go shopping in a real store for once."

"Okay. She might believe that. But how will you check back in?"

"I'll take your sister's number with me, and call her once I'm ready."

"So, what are you shopping for?"

"Some goodies," I answered shortly.

"Yeah, but what kind?"

"The kind everybody likes."

Tee still looked puzzled. "What kind is that?"

I looked up and saw Mrs. Library Grinch on her way, and thought, Thank goodness!

"Look," I said, pointing. There's Fee-Fee coming with the librarian.

This bitch had the nerve to say, "Where? I don't see her."

After picking my mouth up off the ground, I shook my head then turned my attention toward the librarian as she beckoned me. I got up and bid Tee good day before following the librarian inside.

I actually looked forward to chatting with Wayne. He made me feel like I had somewhat of a friend on the outside, even though he was 4786 miles away. I knew the distance because I researched London. I had to know the distance I'd be flying, and I wanted to know the time difference. London was six hours ahead of Central Standard Time—my time. Wayne had never mentioned his time zone, but at least I was aware of it.

Once again, I was the only one in the computer room, but the ol' library Grinch hinted that others would join me soon. I wasn't looking forward to anyone being in the room, but me. I wanted to chat with Wayne in private. I had a lot pinned up, and I wanted to express myself freely and openly.

When Wayne's log-in popped up, I was too excited. I didn't want to seem anxious so I waited for him to reach out to me. And he did.

> HEY YOU, he typed.
> HEY YOURSELF.
> YOU OK?
> YEAH. YOU?
> I'M FINE. MISSING YOU THOUGH. CAME BACK THE OTHER DAY, AND YOU WERE GONE. ☹
> SORRY. HAD TO LEAVE. TRIED TO WARN YOU.
> THAT'S OKAY. I STILL LIKE YOU.
> LIKE? NOT LONG AGO YOU SAID YOU WERE FALLING IN LOVE.
> I SAID I THINK SO. ANYWAY FALLING AND FELL ARE TWO DIFFERENT THINGS.
> OH, WELL, EXCUSE ME.
> DO I DETECT AN ATTITUDE?
> NO, FOR WHAT?
> OH, NOW YOU'RE SASSING ME.
> WHATEVER.
> WHAT'S WRONG, BABE?

Babe? He hadn't called me that in a while. I loved when he called me babe. I suddenly lost the attitude and became nicer.

> I'M OK. I GUESS I'M JUST A LITTLE FRUSTRATED.
> DO I HAVE SOMETHING TO DO WITH THAT?
> NO. BUT YOU MIGHT BE ABLE TO HELP.

ALISHA YVONNE

REALLY? HOW SO?
I'M READY TO SEE YOU.

There was a lapse in the time he responded. I was beginning to think I'd scared him, and then he replied.

KARMA, WE'VE BEEN THROUGH THIS, RIGHT?
WHAT HAPPENED TO BABE? I LIKE THAT BETTER.
OK, BABE. ☺ LET'S NOT GO BACK AND FORTH ABOUT SEEING EACH OTHER RIGHT NOW.
DON'T YOU WANT TO SEE ME?
OF COURSE I DO.
THEN, LET'S MEET AT THE PEABODY HOTEL HERE IN MEMPHIS.
BABE, I'M STILL IN LONDON.
AND?
AND I'M SURE I WOULD LIKE THE PEABODY HOTEL. I HEAR IT'S A BEAUTY, BUT NOW ISN'T A GOOD TIME.
NOT NOW, I answered. SATURDAY.
DO YOU KNOW HOW FAR AWAY I AM?
YES, AND YOU COULD BE HERE IN A COUPLE OF HOURS OR SO ON YOUR PRIVATE JET.
YOU DON'T UNDERSTAND.
NO, YOU DON'T UNDERSTAND.
WHAT DON'T I UNDERSTAND, BABE?
I'M HORNY.

Wayne's response was delayed once again, and that concerned me. I wondered if I had been too forward. I was about to ask if he was still there, but then a message came through.

WOW, BABE, WISH I COULD HELP YOU WITH THAT.

YOU CAN.

WHAT DO YOU WANT FROM ME?

I WANT YOU HERE, BUT IN THE MEANWHILE, DON'T YOU WANT TO KNOW WHAT COLOR PANTIES I'M WEARING?

YES. I WOULD LOVE TO KNOW.

I'M NOT WEARING ANY.

MMM. TELL ME MORE.

I'M RUBBING MY CLIT, AND I'M IMAGINING YOUR TONGUE THERE.

WAIT. YOU'RE TAKING ME TOO FAST. DO YOU HAVE ANYTHING ELSE ON?

YEAH. I'M WEARING A FORM-FITTING TOP WITH A BRIGHT RED BRA UNDERNEATH. WOULD YOU LIKE FOR ME TO TAKE IT OFF?

YES, PLEASE.

OK. DONE. NOW YOU SHOULD SEE MY NIPPLES. THEY'RE ROCK HARD THROUGH MY TOP. WANNA SUCK THEM?

OH YEAH.

MMM. YOU'RE GOOD, WAYNE. I WANNA SUCK YOU, TOO. ARE YOU WET?

EXTREMELY. ARE YOU HARD YET?

YES. EXTREMELY.

WANNA FUCK ME?

YES.

I'M BENDING OVER. COME GET IT FROM THE BACK.

It was a good thing I was only acting on my side of the computer because Wayne had completely disappeared. I waited a short while for a response, and then I was ready to log off. What was he doing? I wondered. I decided to wait. I thought perhaps he became overly excited and had to relieve himself. What was a woman to do—just wait. And then he was back.

STILL THERE? he typed.

I WAS ABOUT TO ASK YOU THE SAME THING.

SORRY. YOU'RE COMMENT DID SOMETHING TO ME.

YEAH, AND NOW I WANT YOU TO DO SOMETHING TO ME.

OK.

IN PERSON.

YOU KEEP SAYING THAT.

I'LL MEET YOU AT THE PEABODY HOTEL SATURDAY.

YOU CAN'T DO THAT.

I was a bit taken aback by his comment. Why would he say I couldn't? He didn't know my circumstance, being on lockdown at the mental facility. I was almost too scared to ask him, but I felt I needed to.

WHAT DO YOU MEAN, WAYNE?

I MEAN, THE PEABODY IS AN AWFULLY EXPENSIVE HOTEL.

YOU CAN AFFORD IT, RIGHT?

ABSOLUTELY.

THEN WHAT'S THE PROBLEM?

THERE'S NO PROBLEM.

GREAT. SATURDAY AT NOON, IT IS. NOW WHERE WERE WE? OH, I REMEMBER. I WAS BENT OVER, AND YOU WERE ABOUT TO FUCK ME FROM BEHIND.

Lawrence

15

---

*T*he phone rang, but I was so wrapped up into my computer screen, I hadn't distinguished whether it was my cell phone or the office phone. I lifted my cell to my ear and answered.

"True Hope," I said, blinking at my monitor.

"True Hope?" Aisha said.

I quickly snapped out of my daze and turned my attention to my wife. "Oh, I mean, hello."

"I see somebody is working hard."

"Um, yeah, I am." I minimized the webpage. "Did you need something, Aisha?"

"Need something? Since when did I need a reason to call and check up on your day?"

"Oh, I get it: You're just looking for a reason to argue."

"No, that's not it, and if you're busy, you could just tell me, instead of asking me if I need something."

I loved my wife, but she was starting to frustrate the hell out of me. It was extremely hard keeping her happy these days. She fussed about any and everything. I knew she wanted to have a baby, but I couldn't make that happen on demand no more than she could. I got the sense that until she could begin her fertility treatments and become pregnant, we would have enough arguments to keep us from feeling and understanding the real love we had for each other. At this moment, I was starting to feel like I didn't want to hear from her or be around her until it was absolutely necessary—like when I had to go home.

Unknowingly, I tuned her out and returned my attention to the webpage I'd been reading. I didn't realize Aisha was still talking until she called my name.

"Dr. Weisman, are you there?"

"Huh? Um, yeah, Aisha, I'm here. I was just listening."

"You don't sound like it."

"Well, sweetie, tell me: What does listening sound like?"

"Don't get smart with me, Larry. You know what I'm saying."

"Aisha, did you ever check into those fertility treatments?"

"Yeah, why?"

"I just asked, sweetie, that's all."

"No, you asked for a reason. So, why did you ask?"

"Okay, listen. I'm going to hang up now because—"

"No, don't hang up, Larry. Just answer the question."

"Aisha, I think we established at the beginning of the call that I was in the middle of working on something, right?" I remained as calm as I could.

"Oh, so now you want to put this on me!"

"Put what on you?" Now I was really frustrated. "Look, I'll talk to you when I get home. Bye!"

I hated that I hung up on Aisha, but not so much so that I wanted to call her back. I'm sure my hanging up stunned her just as much as it did me. The fact that she didn't call back let me know she was getting ready for all-out war once I got home. I needed some place to chill until late night—give her time to cool off.

Cooling off was what I needed, too. As I sat in my office, trying to shake thoughts of Karma and the things we once did, I had a rise like no other. I tried finding things on the Internet to distract me and override my wicked thoughts, but nothing helped. Neither did Aisha's call help. In fact, being mad at her gave me a mind to go ahead and see Karma—given my wife's tendency to put me on and off of punishment. Sex had become a thing of control for Aisha as she rationed it as she saw fit. This was assed backwards for a woman who wanted to have babies, if you asked me.

The more I told myself not to do it, the more I wanted Karma, and I needed her bad. I glanced at the clock on the wall then picked up the receiver to the desk phone. Karma would still be in the computer room, so I dialed the librarian.

"Would you have an officer escort Ms. Jolley to my office, please?" I asked in a mild but urgent tone.

"Yes, sir. Will do," she answered.

This was Darla's off day, and Steve was out to lunch. What could it hurt to just sit behind my desk and look at her? I told myself. *Maybe if I just laid eyes on her, and then jacked off once she left, I would be over this phase.* I wondered what kind of psychiatrist I had become. Not only did I disregard what seeing Karma could do to her, but I even blocked out what it could do to me.

When the knock came to the door, I started to yell for the officer to take Karma away. I didn't want to raise suspicion, so I just told them to come in.

Karma walked in as if she was at home and sat on the couch. I didn't move from my desk. I typed a few lines on the computer as I asked the officer to close the door behind him. After the door closed, I told myself not to even look at Karma. She wasn't having that though.

"Doc, did you call me in here just to let me sit on your couch while you peck away on the computer?"

"Of course not, Karma," I answered, staring at the screen.

"Then, what's up?"

I didn't answer her, nor did I look at her. I just needed to buy a few more minutes of time, and then I could send her away without any of the staff thinking something was wrong.

I could see Karma shift her hip and cross one leg over the other in my peripheral vision. What was surprising to me was that it seemed as if she had on a skirt because I could tell her legs were bare. I knew if she wore a skirt, she more than likely wore nothing under it. I stopped typing momentarily, to focus on her top in my peripheral. It was tight-fitting, and Lord knows if she wasn't wearing a bra, I wasn't going to be able to contain myself.

She has to be wearing a bra, I told myself. The librarian and security wouldn't have let her come to my office without one. I glanced up quickly, hoping Karma wouldn't catch me. But she did.

Karma stared at me and flashed a slight smile. "Doc, you seem nervous. What's wrong?"

I watched my fingers as I pretended to be in deep with something I had to type. "Nothing's wrong, Karma."

"Then why am I in here?"

"I thought I would have time to discuss your upcoming sessions, but as you can see I'm very busy."

"Hmph. Yeah, so busy, you can't even look at me."

I heard her snide remark, but I stayed focused on my pretend typing session and my monitor that was in hibernation. Another minute went by, and then I attempted to release her.

"Well, Karma, I'm sorry I pulled you from what you were doing. I guess we'll have to pick this up another time." I didn't know I could make my fingers dance so much as I spoke.

"What?" she snapped. "So, you're not even going to tell me when our next session is?"

"Um, no. Sorry, Karma. I'll let you know tomorrow. I promise."

"Look at me!" she yelled.

I said nothing—just typed. I could see her starting toward me, and that forced me to look.

"What are you doing?"

"I said look at me," she demanded, cupping my chin as we stared into each other's eyes. "Why are you ignoring me? You know I hate that."

I removed her hand from my face. "I'm sorry. I didn't mean to."

"What are you working on?" She shook my mouse, trying to get my screen to show. "And why is the screen-saver on?"

"Stop that," I said. "I have it set to hibernate when I'm not typing," I lied.

"Liar! You don't want me to see what you're doing."

"Karma, I think it's time for you to leave."

I felt a sense of relief when she sashayed toward the door. I figured she was on her way out, and the officer would just follow her as she fussed down the hall as she'd done before. But that wasn't Karma's plan. She locked the door then turned to me.

"I'm not going anywhere until you give me a reason to leave happy."

She lifted her skirt above her waist, exposing her hairless twat as she seemed to glide over to me. I was beyond speechless. I was thunderstruck and unable to move as my eyes were fixated on what I felt I needed.

She stood in front of me then propped a foot on the arm of my chair. This was the first time I noticed she was wearing a low-heeled strappy sandal. Her toes were polished bright red, and that was sexy as hell. She began to stroke herself and breathe in erotic huffs. She stared into my eyes as she spoke.

"You want to taste this, don't you?" She moaned lightly. "I know you do, Doc. You miss this."

I grabbed her moist hand and began to slowly lick each finger, hoping that would chase away the urge to screw her. But it didn't. The more she talked to me, the more I felt I had to be inside of her.

"Tell me you miss this," she said, winding her hips and stroking her clit with the other hand. "You want this, don't you, Doc?"

"Yeah, I want it." Was that me? Did I really say that out loud?

Apparently, the voice I'd heard was mine, and Karma heard it, too, because before I knew it, she had balanced herself on both arms of my chair and lowered her delectable, honey pot into my face. I gripped her ass and held her to me until she began to tremble uncontrollably and begged for me to stop. She almost screamed out a time or two.

Once she got down from my chair, she attempted to help me get ready, but there was no need. I was hard as a brick, and I almost felt sorry for her. I bent her over my desk then entered her with so much drive, she had to use one hand to hold on to the desk and cup her mouth with the other.

Shortly after I released, I lay on her back, winded and relieved. I was just about to get up when I heard the doorknob turning back and forth, and then heavy knocking.

"Dr. Weisman, I need to speak to you," I heard Darla Mitchell say.

I jumped and pulled up my pants. Karma's eyes were just as wide as mine. She mouthed a question of what we should do. My mind was spinning. I had no answers.

Darla shouldn't have been at work. Last I checked, it was her day off. Perhaps she had been called in. All I knew was I didn't need for Darla to come into my office at that moment. I was sweating like a Hebrew slave, and there might've even been a stench of sex in the air. I had to figure out how to get her away from my door, and I'd be lucky if I could get Karma back to the library without Darla ever knowing she was there.

KNOCK. KNOCK. KNOCK.

"Dr. Weisman, I need to speak to you—and Karma. The librarian said she was here."

There went my luck.

Karma

16

If it wasn't for bad luck, some people just wouldn't have luck at all. Poor Doc couldn't seem to have luck on his side even if he had paid for it. Two days ago, just after Doc released the orgasm of his life, Nurse Mitchell showed up at his office, knocking like she was the police with a search warrant for me. How the hell she had decided to come up to the center on her off day to discuss my meds were beyond me. In my opinion, she could've called that information in to the nurse in charge, or else that shit could've waited.

Doc had me go into the restroom in his office to freshen up. I turned and noticed him wiping his forehead and face with some Kleenex he'd pulled from a box on his desk. As he started toward the door, I went into the restroom and locked it. I stood quiet, listening for what Nurse Mitchell had to say.

Nurse Mitchell didn't seem interested in talking to Doc at all. In fact, I heard her voice calling out to me the moment he opened his door.

"She's in the restroom," I heard Doc say. "Is there something I can help you with?"

"What's she doing in the restroom," Nurse Mitchell had asked.

"Oh, I don't know . . . perhaps the same thing other people do in restrooms. Look, I'm busy. What's so important?"

She gave him some little spiel about having forgotten to mention another med I'd taken since my stay there, and she thought it was important he and I knew I had a prescription missing. Doc didn't sound as if he believed her reasoning for the urgency, but he let her off the hook with a nice tone and suggested she really didn't need to come there for that.

I stepped out of the restroom and spoke. Nurse Mitchell gave me a once-over, smirked then turned to leave. I really didn't know where she got off, giving me that behavior. I made sure I looked fine before I left the restroom. Doc shook his head for me not to say anything until she was gone. He never did explain what he thought her attitude was about.

Anyway, it was Saturday—another big day for me. Wayne was on his way to the states to see me. This day almost didn't feel real. Wayne and I hadn't even learned each other's last names, and here we were about to meet. I was a little nervous, but at least I knew what he looked like. He didn't have a clue what to expect of me.

It was hard to believe that I had a rich man—something like a tycoon, interested in me. I had to see how things went on this first date before I could decide whether to continue seeing him. I didn't care about Wayne's riches though. My heart was with Doc. I knew I was slowly gaining his trust, and he'd soon be all mine. Meanwhile, it was okay for me to have a little fun with Wayne, if I wanted to.

I showered, pulled my hair back like Tee's then practiced her annoying laugh in the mirror. She met me on the back lawn, where we swapped clothes behind a set of Blue Point Juniper shrubs.

"Okay, Tee. You know what to do, right?"

"Mm-hmm," she said then giggled.

"No, no, no, Tee. You can't do that giggle. You've got to practice not giggling around people or else they will figure out you're not me, okay?"

"Okay."

This time she just stared at the ground as we'd practiced. I also gave her a cap and sunglasses to wear while she hung outside. I put on my cap and sunglasses, too.

"Now remember, Tee. Don't talk to anyone. Not even Fee-Fee, okay?"

"Okay. I won't."

"And once you go inside, you are not to go into your room."

"Right," she whispered. "I'm going into your room."

"Right."

"What time are you coming back?"

"I'm not sure. Does your sister know I'll need her to pick me back up from the mall?"

"Yeah. I told Josie you're going to Oak Court Mall."

"Good, and I'll give her a call to pick me up when I'm done."

"Oh, can you pick me up something?"

"I don't have much money, Tee. My check hasn't cleared my account yet."

"Well, mine either, but I just wanted something sweet."

"Okay. I'll try to remember. I plan to be back before lockdown, so don't go to sleep. We'll switch rooms when I get back."

"Gotcha."

I peeped around the evergreen shrubs to see if anyone was looking our way. Satisfied they weren't, I sent Tee to the patio with my ear plugs and iPod to pretend to be me. I watched as she sat quietly, looking through my iPod. I was proud of her. I slipped from behind the shrub then entered the building and headed toward the front desk.

"There she is," the receptionist sang.

I saw a woman with a strong resemblance to Tee— and to me at the moment—standing in front of the desk. She had to be Josie. She signed a clip board then stretched her hand toward me as I walked up.

"C'mon, sister, dear," the woman said.

I didn't want to speak, so I waved goodbye to the receptionist and let out one of Tee's ridiculous giggles.

Once in the car, I fastened my seatbelt and told Josie thank you.

"Oh, you don't have to thank me," she said. "You should be thanking my sister. Once she told me your story of not having any family, my heart went out to you. I'm glad I can help."

She went on and on, talking about this and that. I really wanted her to shut up, but I couldn't tell her that. She was doing me a huge favor, and I knew there was no one else who would even consider me and Tee's game, even if I paid them.

When Josie pulled in front of Dillard's, it wasn't soon enough. My ears were ringing from all of the talking she did. I almost jumped out of the car as it slowed in front of the store, but she stopped me.

"Hey, wait, Karma. Let me come to a complete stop. I don't want you to hurt yourself."

I mustered a smile. "Oh, yeah. Right."

"So, do I pick you up here?"

"Yes, ma'am," I answered, trying to be polite. "I'll call you from one of the store phones when I'm ready."

"All right, but remember your curfew."

"What curfew?"

"Don't you need to be back before lockdown?"

"Oh, yes. I'll call you in plenty of time."

"All right. Enjoy."

"Thanks," I said, sliding out of the car.

I went inside the mall and walked around Dillard's for about fifteen minutes or so. I had to make sure Josie was long gone. I also had a few minutes to spare until the

MATA bus would arrive. I had done my research online for the bus schedule, and I asked a passerby where I could catch the bus.

Everything started out working in my favor. My only concern was whether one of the nurses would look for me and discover that Tee was not me. I could only hope they'd leave Tee alone and let her do her thing until I could return. I wished I'd had a cell phone. Wayne knew I didn't have one, so I was sure he'd just be where I told him and keep a look out for me.

The bus let me out on Union Avenue, not far from the Peabody Hotel. It was a beautiful day. Autozone Park seemed larger than I'd remembered, and so did many of the other downtown buildings. It was funny how being housed in a facility like True Hope made me forget what Memphis really looked like. I missed my freedom more than I knew.

I hurried across the street to the Peabody Hotel. I wasn't sure of the time, but I knew it had to be close to noon—time for Wayne and I to meet. I was so excited, entering into the hotel. This place felt rich—like I was out of place, and perhaps I didn't belong. The elegance of it all took my breath away.

I took a seat on a nearby bench and people-watched for a while. I kept an eye out for Wayne. He said he'd be wearing a grey button-down shirt and black slacks, which wouldn't have been hard to spot, but an hour after the time he was supposed to be there, I became worried. All the white men I'd seen either had on suits or white shirts and dark pants.

Two and a half hours later, I was convinced, Wayne would not show. He broke my heart, but at least I still had Doc. It would've been nice to actually meet Wayne, but I pretty much deserved the egg I had on my face. I was no dummy about the fact that this man didn't know me and probably wouldn't fly across waters to meet me. I left True Hope with my mind in the right perspective. I had only hoped he would show up. I really just wanted to get away for a while—see some walls that didn't look like those in True Hope—breathe some air that smelled like something other than Lysol and flowers. And that I did.

Once I stepped outside of The Peabody Hotel, the aroma from TGI Friday's across the street called my name. I was hungry, and I still had time to mess around before going back to the hellhole I was forced to call home. A hostess met me at the door.

"How many in your party today?" she asked.

"Just one," I responded.

She smiled. "Follow me."

I walked closely behind the woman until she stopped at a booth.

"Will this be okay?"

"Yes, this will be just fine."

She handed me a menu then assured me a waitress would be over to take my order shortly. I glanced over the menu, looking for anything to catch my eye. Something caught my eye alright, but it wasn't on the menu. The minute I briefly looked up, I saw a man and a woman seated side-by-side in a booth in the far corner, having what seemed like a serious discussion. I could only see the side of his face, but I was almost sure it was him.

I wanted to do something to get his attention, but I feared giving myself away. What could I do? I had to do something to get him to turn in my direction. I had to know if it was him.

My heart raced in the moments I waited for the man to face me. The woman looked to be near tears. Whatever he was saying to her, she clearly was not happy. She mostly spoke with her hands, and her face was filled with frustration.

When he straightened his body and faced forward, I nearly dropped my menu on the floor. I quickly scooped it from the table and held it in my face, covering everything except my eyes. He stared at his plate. My waitress finally showed up.

"Good afternoon, ma'am," the polite woman said. "I brought you a glass of water, but I'll take your drink order now, if you're ready." She set the glass on the table then poised her pen onto a pad.

"Um . . . um," I said, holding the menu just below my eyes. "Um, you know what. I'm not that hungry. Will you do me a favor and bring me the check for the couple over in the corner?"

She looked over her shoulder. "Oh, do you know them?"

"Um, yes. They're old friends. But do me a favor and don't let them know I'm here. They seem to be in deep conversation, and I don't want to ruin it for them."

"No problem," the woman said just before turning to leave.

It only took her a few minutes to retrieve the tab for Doc's table. She handed it to me then announced she'd be right back. I held the menu in my face with one hand and glared at the receipt in the other hand. It seemed the happy couple had shared the loaded skillet chip nachos as an appetizer. One of them also enjoyed the parmesan-crusted chicken, and the other the Cajun shrimp and chicken pasta.

I eased the menu from my eyes and took another look at them. They were definitely arguing about something—what I couldn't tell. The woman dropped her head and placed her left hand on her forehead. Her wedding set made it painfully obvious that she was Mrs. Lawrence Weisman. She was beautiful, and having come to that realization even hurt. His wife wasn't supposed to be as attractive or more attractive than me.

The waitress returned and collected my money for their tab. I couldn't take my eyes off them. He seemed to love her. He tried to comfort her, rubbing her hair as she openly moped.

The waitress left and returned once again, thanking me for having stopped in. I fanned her away then decided I should get out of there before Doc spotted me. When I saw my waitress heading for their table, I quickly jumped up and headed for the door. I took a peep over my shoulder and saw Doc staring straight at me. I picked up my pace and hoped he wasn't on my tail.

Lawrence

17

---

*D*arla was relentless. She literally became a pain in the ass—texting me, calling, and popping up in my office, demanding we have dinner, so we could talk. She still insisted what she knew about Karma and me. I could imagine what kind of hell she'd give me if I let any more time go by without giving her a response. I called the nurses' station and asked to speak with her.

"Yes, this is Dr. Weisman. I need to speak with Nurse Mitchell, please," I said to the attendant.

It took a minute, but she finally came to the phone. "This is Nurse Mitchell," she said.

"Nurse Mitchell, this is Dr. Weisman."

"Hello, Doctor." I could hear the smile in her voice.

"I trust all is well since we last spoke."

"It is, Doctor. How may I help you?"

"About dinner. When and where do you suppose we meet?"

"That would totally be your call, Doctor." I could tell someone may have been near because she seemed to be speaking in codes.

"Great. Let's say we have dinner tonight, around seven, at Evergreen Grill. Are you familiar with that place? It's on Overton Park."

"Yes. I'm familiar with it."

"Great. I'll see you tonight."

"Thanks, Doctor," she said just before hanging up.

I sat at my desk several minutes thinking of the next call I had to make. That was the conversation I dreaded more than anything—the talk with my wife. Aisha would not be thrilled to hear that I would miss dinner with her yet another night, but I had to do what needed to be done.

I called Aisha and had the small argument I knew would ensue.

"So, what else is new," Aisha spat just after I gave her the news. "Work always comes first, right?"

"Not always, Aisha."

"Hmph. Why don't you just be frank with me?"

"About what, Aisha?"

"Do you even still want this marriage?"

"Do I even still, what the hell—yeah! Yeah, baby. Look. Don't do this."

"I mean, Larry, it seems to me your other woman keeps standing in our way. Why don't you just be with her and leave me alone?" Her voice trembled.

I sighed. "Baby, I'm not—" I cut myself off. "Aisha, listen to me. I'm where I want to be. You hear me?" There was a moment of silence and then she sniffled. "Baby, don't be talking about divorce or me leaving you because that's never going to happen. Okay?"

She didn't give me the soft, sweet response I had expected. Instead, she was firm, snappy, and mean.

"Anyway, I'll be fine as *always*," she said without a hint of a tear in her voice. "Do what you do!"

"So, baby, what's the verdict on those fertility treatments? You're still researching, right?" I tried my best to divert the conversation to a place she'd less likely be upset about.

"Yeah."

"And? What did you find out?"

"Nothing we haven't already discussed."

She continued to be cold and brief with me, so I knew it was time to end the call.

"Well, we can talk about it when I get in. I promise not to work too late."

"Whatever," she responded just before hanging up.

Though I didn't like how our call ended, I was glad it was actually over. The only thing left to do was figure out how to get Darla's annoying ass off my back. One thing I knew I would not do, and that was fuck her. I seriously regretted ever sleeping with Darla. Unlike Karma, I could totally resist Darla. She just didn't appeal to me, and when I broke it off with her, I seriously had intentions of staying faithful to my wife.

Steve stopped by my office just as I was about to leave for the day. He tapped on the door only once then walked in.

"Dr. Weisman—working late, are we?" he teased.

"Something like that." I walked over to the coat rack and grabbed my suit jacket.

"It's six o'clock. I know Aisha must be having a fit right now."

I shook my head. "Yeah, you're probably right." I sighed.

"What's wrong, Captain?" He chuckled. "You don't seem to be in a joking mood."

"Man, Aisha and I don't seem to be getting any better, and Lord only knows when she'll be able to get pregnant."

"Damn. Sorry, man."

"And let me tell you: If Aisha's griping, yelling ass isn't enough, how about Darla keeps adding fuel to the fire. She won't leave me alone, man. I mean, I have enough shit stressing me out with trying to get Karma's ass out of here without added pressure from Aisha and Darla."

"I wish I could say I feel for you, man, but the truth is you brought all of this on yourself."

I stood, staring at Steve. He really knew how to kick a man when he was down. The truth always hurt though. I couldn't be mad at him for telling the truth. I grabbed my keys off my desk then headed toward the door.

"So, why are you just now leaving," Steve asked, walking on my heels.

"I was killing time. I've got to meet Darla for dinner."

"Whoa, whoa, whoa," Steve said, grabbing my shoulder.

I stopped and turned to him. "She requested we have dinner to talk. I have to appease her somehow and try to figure out what she wants."

"You know what she wants. She wants you."

"Well, that's not gonna happen."

"Are you sure?"

"Positive!"

"Yeah, and I hope you mean that."

"Trust me. I do. I just want to see how to clear the smoke in the air between us, and hopefully, get her off my back about Karma. She keeps insisting she knows what's up. I have to make her believe nothing unethical has taken place between Karma and me."

"Well, good luck. Damn, I'm glad I've got more sense than you," Steve said, pushing me out of my own office.

"Kiss my ass," I spat just after looking around to make sure no one else would hear me. "Move out my way. I need to lock the door."

Steve threw his hands up then walked around me with a smirk.

"Oh, yeah? Well, I love you, too, bro'," he said with a chuckle. "And I'll still help you in any way I can."

"A'ight."

I threw him a peace sign then headed for the parking garage. I wasn't looking forward to dinner with Darla. The sooner we met, the sooner we could get it over with. I thought of all the things I'd say to her on the drive over to Evergreen Grill. I wanted to be prepared for whatever she could throw at me.

I parked on the side of the restaurant, but I could still see the entrance. It was a clear, tranquil evening in May. The sky was blue with patches of red and orange streaks, hinting the sun was about to set. Two-person tables with couples having candlelight dinners lined the sidewalk just in front of the restaurant. They all seemed happy—drama-free, in fact. That's how I needed my life to be. And I would get back my peace at any cost.

When I saw Darla walking up the sidewalk, I took a deep breath then turned off the radio in my car. She entered without looking back to notice me getting out of my car. I took several more deep breaths, trying to relax before I would be sitting down at a table in front of her.

A waitress gave me a warm greeting once I entered, and then asked if someone would be joining me.

"Um, yes," I answered, looking around for Darla. She fanned me over to her table. "Oh, there she is."

The waitress and I headed over to Darla's table. She sat near the window at a two-person table. I ordered wine for both of us and asked the waitress to give us a minute to place our orders. She was very kind to do so.

Darla was dressed in a black, fitted dress with black pumps and silver accessories. Her hair looked nice, too. She wore it down with big lose curls. I could see she put some thought into the dinner with me. I got the impression she wanted it to be more like a date, and I guess anyone looking at us could probably assume that because I was dressed in the black slacks, white shirt and tie that I wore to work. I dismissed the awkward silence that lingered over us.

"So, Darla, how was your afternoon?"

"Not bad," she answered, staring at me seductively.

I nodded, thinking the waitress needed to bring me something stronger than a glass of wine. I had a feeling Darla was looking for something more than dinner to eat. I cleared my throat then glanced around the restaurant.

"This little place is cozy. I've been here once with Aisha. She liked it, too."

"Is that right?" Her eyes were glued to mine. "Well, I'm glad you suggested it. I love a cozy environment, too."

My throat was no longer just dry—it was parched. I swallowed hard, trying to relieve the burn in my esophagus. The waitress finally walked up with our wine. I took two long gulps then insisted she bring me another glass. The waitress nodded then headed toward the kitchen. I turned my attention to Darla.

"So, Darla, what is it that's so important that we couldn't discuss it at my office?"

"Well, Lawrence. I figured we had to talk about some things we needed closure on."

"Like what?"

"Like our baby."

I was taken aback. We didn't need to discuss a child because there was no child between us. "Come again," I said politely.

"The baby you asked me to abort."

"What about it?"

"Lawrence, I offered to do so because I loved you. I believed we could maintain some type of relationship."

"Darla, what part of married do you not understand about me? I admit: What we did was wrong, and I surely didn't expect you to get pregnant. But, I never wanted to just run around on my wife and especially have a baby in the mix of things. I thought you understood that."

"So, if you're this faithful man you say you are, why then are you sleeping around with your mentally-ill patient?"

A lump formed in my throat. I picked up the second glass of wine the waitress brought to me then took a gulp. I had to give her an answer. I was cornered in a restaurant with her. It wasn't like we were in my office and I could just tell her I was busy and would get back to her. I was careful not to put on the defense though.

"Darla, are we going to talk, or are we going to throw accusations at each other all night? I would rather have a discussion."

She sipped her wine then set the glass on the table. "You're right. I much rather talk." She picked up her menu. "I think I'm ready to order."

"So am I."

I beckoned the waitress over then ordered the first pasta dish that caught my eye.

"I'll have the chicken tortellini, please," I told the waitress.

"And I'll have the garlic rosemary chicken, please," Darla stated.

As soon as the waitress was gone, I came right out and demanded answers from Darla.

"Why are we really here?" I asked.

"What do you mean?" she answered innocently.

"Darla, I don't want to play games. I want to get to the bottom of why meeting me was so important. I mean, I don't mind having this dinner with you," I lied, "but, let's not beat around the bush here. You want something. So tell me. What is it?"

At first she dropped her head, and then she glanced up at me and said, "You haven't paid attention to me since we've been here."

"Huh?"

"I can see I'm of no significance to you."

"What are you saying?"

"Here I am—out of uniform—in a very nice dress and red lipstick—something you aren't accustomed to from me, but you still don't see me."

I sighed heavily. Now she was getting to where I sort of knew she'd go with the conversation. Before I could say anything, she cut me off.

"Am I annoying you, Lawrence?"

"I'm not annoyed, Darla," I said, lying once more. "I just don't see why this is the conversation you want to have. If I were a man looking to mess around on his wife, I would be glad to offer you all the compliments in the world."

"I've never gotten over you. I know what we had was brief, but for the little time it was, it felt real. You made me feel wanted. And it kills me knowing you might be sleeping with Jolley."

"Darla, I—"

"Listen. I know you don't want to hear accusations, and you're just going to keep denying it, but I can see it in her eyes. She comes away from you with the same look on her face I did when I thought you cared for me."

"Can we at least agree on one thing?"

"What's that?"

"That you're just going on what you think and not what you know."

"Sure. I have no proof. My gut tells me I'm right though."

I shook my head. "What would make you happy, Darla?"

She gave me a knowing-glance then rolled her eyes. It was time for both of us to have a sip from our glasses. She set her glass down, took a deep breath then said it.

"I want to play around from time to time."

"Darla—"

"Wait. I'm not finished. I know you're married. I'm only asking for a little of your time. I would never ask you to leave your wife. But I do want you to leave Karma alone. She doesn't deserve the false attention you're giving her. Send her to a doctor who will give her the treatment she needs."

I was just about stumped for words. "Wow. I don't know what to say. I guess I can start by just letting you know that Ms. Jolley won't be in my care for much longer, but it's not for the reasons you're thinking. And next, in regard to you and me, I guess I could at least think about it."

"Fine. Since I'm just springing this on you, I guess I can agree to that."

"But let me ask you something. What if I come back and tell you I just can't go through with an affair?"

"Hmm," she said then sat back in her chair. "Then, I guess I will be forced to do what I didn't want to over the years."

I frowned. "What's that?"

"Take you and your wife to juvenile court."

I couldn't believe my ears. I knew she had put on some weight back then, but she swore to me she had the abortion. Why didn't I follow my instincts that told me to follow her to that clinic? A child? With Darla? Aisha would not only divorce me—she would kill me.

Karma

18

I'd been feeling down ever since Wayne didn't show up to meet me. I knew in all likelihood he wouldn't show, but I could only hope. I didn't expect to feel so crossed about it though. Or, maybe my feelings were mixed with emotions from having seen Doc and his beautiful wife. I don't know what I expected, but I really didn't think a man with a woman as gorgeous as Mrs. Weisman could even be tempted to have an affair with someone else. *What the hell did he want with me?* I wondered. Obviously, I brought something to the table she didn't.

I was done questioning myself and my relationship with Doc. He wanted me, and that was all that mattered. As for Wayne, I hadn't made up my mind when I would speak to him again. It was now Tuesday—my computer day, but I wasn't in the mood for chatting with Wayne. He knew my schedule and would be expecting me to be online soon, but I wasn't going to the computer room. Maybe it was his turn to suffer waiting on me. In fact, he might have to wait on me all week. He had to suffer somehow, and I didn't know any other way to make him pay other than by me not showing up online.

Tee came over and offered to play cards.

"Go Fish?" she asked, giggling and waving the deck of cards at me.

I nodded. "Sure. Why not?"

"I'm so glad we're friends, Karma."

"You are?"

"Yeah, and my sister says she's glad, too. She said it made her feel good to be able to do that favor for you." She let out her famous giggle again.

"In that case, I'm glad we're friends, too. You tell your sister I may need her again real soon."

"I will."

Tee had just shuffled the cards when Nurse Mitchell walked over to us on the lawn.

"Hi Teresa. Hi Karma," she said, smiling.

"Hello, Nurse Mitchell," Tee answered then giggled.

I didn't speak. I didn't even look at her at first. Nurse Mitchell never came out on the lawn just to speak to us, so something told me she was about to irk my nerves.

"What are you ladies doing?" Nurse Mitchell asked.

"We're about to play Go Fish," Tee answered. "Wanna play?"

"NO!" I screamed before I knew it. "I mean, Nurse Mitchell doesn't have time to play cards with us, Tee. What's wrong with you? She has other things to do. Don't you, Nurse Mitchell?"

"Well, Karma, if I didn't know any better, I'd say you don't want me to play with you all." Her hands were on her hips now.

I didn't answer. I just watched the cards while Tee dealt. I picked mine up and sorted them in my hand.

"Karma didn't mean anything like that," Tee answered for me. "She just doesn't want to take up your time." More giggling escaped her lips.

"Oh, okay. That makes sense," Nurse Mitchell said.

Tee set the deck down then picked up her cards to straighten them. Nurse Mitchell interrupted our game before we could begin.

"Um, Teresa, before you start, may I speak with Karma alone?"

"For how long?" Tee frowned. "We were just about to play."

"I know. I promise not to take long. I just need a brief minute with her. You can go over to that bench over with your friend, um, what's her name?" Nurse Mitchell asked.

"Fee-Fee," Tee yelled.

"That's right . . . Fee-Fee. I'll come and get you guys when I'm done." Nurse Mitchell gave her pleading eyes.

"Well, alright. But don't take too long. Karma will be going to the computer room soon."

Tee got up and took her hand and the deck with her. We hadn't even started the game, and besides, why would I want to cheat in a game of Go Fish when there wasn't even any money involved. I shook my head and watched as she walked away. Nurse Mitchell didn't even begin her conversation until she was satisfied Tee was sitting on the bench across the lawn. She sat in the seat next to me.

"So, how have you been, Karma."

"I'm great, and you?"

"Good. I'm doing great as well."

"So, what's this about, Nurse Mitchell?"

"Well . . . I just wanted to chat a bit. We don't get to talk much these days."

"We never talk, so what's really going on?" I snapped.

"Okay, Karma. You're a smart girl. I guess I should just come out and ask you."

"Ask me what?"

"Is there anything going on between you and Dr. Weisman?"

I hadn't been looking at her, but she had my undivided attention at that point. The nerve of this lady was incredible. How dare she ask me such a question!

"Excuse me?" I said calmly.

"Has Dr. Weisman ever did or said anything inappropriate to you?"

"Absolutely not," I answered in my appalled voice. "What would make you imply something like that?"

"I just had a hunch—"

"A hunch?" I cut her off. "You would challenge that man's integrity on a hunch?"

"Well, it's just that—"

"Just what? Are you fucking him?"

"Karma!"

"Well, you insulted me first. How dare you come ask if I'm whoring around with my doctor, and then pretend to be shocked when I'm offended."

"I didn't mean to offend you. I'm only trying to protect you. You deserve the best care possible while you're in this facility. I just care about your wellbeing, that's all."

"Well, I'm fine."

"Okay," she responded in a tender tone.

"And the doctor is a professional *and* a gentleman."

"Okay."

"I would appreciate if you never come to me with something like this again."

"Karma, it's okay to tell me the truth, you know?"

I looked at her sideways. "Did you not just hear what I said?"

"I heard you. I just want you to know—between me and you—if he ever crosses the line with you, I'm in your corner."

"What makes you think he'd ever cross the line?"

I could see the gulp in her throat as she swallowed before answering, "He crossed the line with me once."

Perhaps she saw the steam coming from my ears—I wasn't sure, but she slowly stood before she finished what she had to say.

"It's not fair when men of position and power take advantage of us, and often we feel alone and like we have no one to talk to. I was in your shoes once."

"You were his mental patient?" I asked sarcastically.

"No. I was just a nurse, but I felt he cared about me. Why else would I have let him undress me?"

"You had sex with him?" I was stunned.

She nodded. "Karma, I'm only sharing this with you because I want you to be careful. If you say he's being professional with you, I believe you. Just make sure it remains that way. I don't want you to end up hurt like me. Let's just keep this little talk between you and me, okay?"

I dropped my head. "Okay."

"And if you ever need to talk about anything with me, I'm here for you, all right?"

"Thanks."

She walked away and into the building. My blood was boiling. Doc was a straight up player. He did something I said I wouldn't let him do—play me. Nobody plays me. Tee walked back over.

"Heeeyyy," she said. "I thought Nurse Mitchell said she was going to come get me when she was finished."

I was so distraught I couldn't speak. I knew Nurse Mitchell was up to something when she showed up. I just had no idea she was about to break that kind of news to me. Now everything made sense—her attitude with me on the days I met with Doc, her popping up during our meetings, especially on her off day—it all made perfect sense. Maybe they were *still* screwing. Maybe that was her real issue. I couldn't take anymore speculating. I had to know.

"I'll be back," I told Tee as I suddenly jumped up.

"You going to the computer room?"

"No. Just hold on. I'll be back."

"Where're you going?"

I ignored Tee's last question as I stormed into the building and headed straight for Doc's office. I expected to see Nurse Mitchell on the way, but I didn't see her. As a matter of fact, no one seemed to even notice me until I made it in front of his door. One of the security officers asked where I was going without an escort. I heard him, and at the same time, I didn't. My mind was focused on getting inside Doc's office.

I turned the knob, and to my relief, the door opened. Doc sat behind his desk on the phone. The security officer who questioned me was right on my tail.

"What are you doing here?" the officer asked, grabbing my arm. "No one told me you needed an escort."

"That's because I don't, you moron," I turned to him and said. "Let me go!" I jerked from him.

Doc's mouth was wide open for a second, and then he got rid of his caller. "Hey, listen. I have a situation going on here. Let me call you back," he said into the phone.

"Get off of me!" I screamed at the officer.

"Is it okay, Dr. Weisman?" he asked.

"Yes. Let her go."

The officer released me then backed out of the office. As I ran over to Doc, his eyes widened and he stood, seemingly realizing I was out for blood.

WHAM! He tried to duck, but my open palm caught him right across the face. I drew back to swat at him again, but he grabbed both of my wrists.

"Let me go, asshole! Let me go!" I was furious.

"Karma, what's wrong with you?"

"You're fucking her!" I said, wrestling to free my wrists. "It all makes sense."

"What makes sense?"

"Nurse Mitchell . . . she's been popping up and acting strange because you're screwing her!"

"Where'd you get that from?"

"She told me! Where else would I get it from?"

He sighed and rolled his eyes. "Karma, she's playing you. She's been suspicious of us for a while now. She just wanted to see what kind of information she could get out of you. She played that game with me, too."

I stopped tussling long enough to listen. I was just about out of breath.

"So you've never had sex with her?"

"Karma, I'm going to be honest with you. Yes, I did, but it was only once, and that happened a long time ago. I'm not fooling around with Nurse Mitchell. She may still have eyes for me, but I don't want her."

He loosened his grip, and I jerked from him.

"Do you know she came out on the lawn and confronted me with the news flash that she's had you?"

"I don't know what to say about that except I'm sorry she did that to you. I have no desire to mess around with Nurse Mitchell. It just kind of happened several years ago, and I've regretted it ever since. You've got to believe me."

I took a deep breath. I believed him, but this also meant Nurse Mitchell would have to go under my radar. Any woman who wanted my man had to be dealt with accordingly.

Lawrence

19

---

*I*t was such a pleasant surprise and change of pace in my marriage for Aisha to offer to take me out. I had told her the night before that I cancelled all of my appointments for the next day and took a personal day off—just to rest my mind. Little did she know all that had me spinning— Karma with her foolishness and Darla with even more foolishness. I brought it all on myself, but damn how I never expected things to be so far out of control.

No matter the mess I'd made, my heart was with the woman I married. Aisha offered to cancel her photo shoot at the modeling agency, so we could spend some time together—her treat, and she did so with a smile.

This was the first time she'd paid for anything since I'd met her. It never bothered me that she didn't spend money on me. I did wonder, however, if she ever thought about it. My friends and colleagues would sometimes mention the things their wives did for them on non-holiday days or when it wasn't even their birthdays, and that made me curious as to whether Aisha would ever show me unsolicited attention.

Aisha decided we could do lunch and a movie. She asked what I had a taste for, and after careful consideration, I wanted Italian. We went to Carrabba's in Collerville before the matinee. We hadn't been to a movie in quite a while. I'd rented a few good ones in the previous months, but it felt great looking up at the large Malco Theater screen while sharing popcorn and candy with my wife.

The office had called my cell phone a number of times during the day, but I refused to answer. The entire staff knew well in advance that I'd taken the day off. I did wonder if Karma was behaving though. But, I figured if there had been a problem, someone would have left a message.

Aisha and I returned home around 4:30 in the afternoon. We still had a lot of hours ahead of us to do whatever we wanted, and she made it plain just how she wanted to spend the rest of the evening.

"Honey, I was thinking I could go run us some water in the Jacuzzi and fix a couple of glasses of champagne. What do you think?" she asked just after entering our home through the kitchen.

"Hmm. Let me think," I answered, placing my finger on my temple. "Does this Jacuzzi bath come with a massage and intense sex?"

Aisha was all smiles. "And you know it!" She giggled then walked closer to me. "I've started the fertility pills the doctor gave me, so we've got a baby to make, remember?"

"Mm-hmm. I remember."

We kissed long and hard. It felt good to share a kiss with her once again that came from nothing but love. I could tell she felt the same way. Each time I tried to break away, she stuck her tongue farther into my mouth. I finally just had to speak through her kisses.

"Sweetie, let's save some for the Jacuzzi," I managed to say.

She pulled away. "Okay. Give me ten minutes to set everything up."

"Sure," I said then placed a soft peck on her lips. "I'm going to check my email in that time—you know, to make sure everything is all right at the office."

"Oh, that's right. Someone has been calling you. You never answered?"

"No, and it must not have been important. No one left a message. Besides, I was where I wanted to be—with my baby."

"Aaaaww," she crooned. "Well, that makes two of us. Let me hurry, so we can do what grown folks do." She smiled then winked.

"Yeah. I won't be online very long. We'll pick up this hot date in the Jacuzzi in ten minutes flat."

"I'll meet you there."

We kissed one more time for good measure, but it was a brief exchange. Aisha headed down the hall, toward our bedroom. I headed for my home office.

My computer was still up from earlier, so all I had to do was check my inbox. There were several messages from Karma. I dared not open any because I could only imagine what they would say. My day had been magnificent up to that point, and there was no way I would let Karma ruin it.

I glanced at the second browser on the screen. It displayed the eLovers Row website. I had pulled it up that morning to see if I could notice anything suspicious from Karma, but I didn't find anything. She had no idea I'd known about her frequenting that site since she first began. I never mentioned it to her because I needed a way to keep up with what she was doing online without her suspecting me watching her. Confident she had behaved herself all day, I decided to close the site. I stretched my cursor over the red box with the "x," but I was caught by surprise when a message popped up from TrueRedKarma.

WHAT ARE YOU DOING ONLINE, LIAR? she typed.

HUH? ME? A LIAR? I responded.

YEAH, YOU. I DIDN'T EXPECT YOU BACK ON HERE ANY TIME SOON.

AND WHY IS THAT?

BECAUSE YOU'RE A COWARD. YOU COULDN'T EVEN FACE ME!

She seemed furious about something, and her last comment really confused me. What was she talking about, and what was she doing in the computer room so late? I knew Aisha was expecting me, but I had to get to the bottom of things with this girl because she had to be up to something.

I WANT TO KNOW WHAT YOU'RE ACCUSING ME OF, BUT FIRST, WHAT ARE YOU DOING ONLINE AT THIS HOUR?

WHAT DO YOU MEAN?

I'VE NEVER SEEN YOU HERE THIS LATE.

PERHAPS YOU HADN'T LOOKED HARD ENOUGH THEN.

Could she just be talking smack? I had extended her time in the computer room to pacify her, but still, I'd never seen her online pass 3:00 P.M. My mind raced with thoughts of how to get answers from her without giving myself away.

OH. WELL I GUESS I DIDN'T, HUH? I typed.

JUST LIKE THE DAY YOU STOOD ME UP.

WAIT. ARE YOU SERIOUS?

YES, I'M SERIOUS. AND YOU DIDN'T EVEN CARE HOW THAT WOULD MAKE ME FEEL.

At this point, I just knew Karma was calling my bluff. Her so-called WhiteKnight lived in London, and she had no means of leaving the institution, so she must've known the man on the other side of the screen wouldn't show up, right? I decided to play her game.

BABE, YOU HAVE GOT TO BE KIDDING ME. WHAT ABOUT MY FEELINGS?

EXCUSE ME? she responded. NOW WHAT ARE YOU TALKING ABOUT?

MISS LADY, MEN HAVE FEELINGS, TOO, AND IT DIDN'T FEEL GOOD TO HAVE YOU STAND ME UP.

WAYNE, STOP PLAYING GAMES. YOU NEVER SHOWED UP. I KNOW BECAUSE I WAS THERE.

YOU WERE WHERE? This really piqued my curiosity.

AT THE PEABODY LIKE WE DISCUSSED.

Hmm, I thought. *So she still wants to play this game, I see.* I continued to call her bluff.

WELL, I WAS THERE, TOO, I responded.

REALLY?

YES, REALLY. HOW DID WE MISS EACH OTHER?

I DON'T KNOW. I WAITED AND WAITED ON YOU.

MAYBE I HAD THE TIME MIXED UP OR SOMETHING. ALL I KNOW IS I WAS THERE. I'M SORRY I DIDN'T GET TO SEE YOU.

ME, TOO. AND I'M SORRY I CALLED YOU A LIAR.

THAT'S OK, BABE.

LET'S START THIS CONVERSATION OVER, she offered.

OK. BUT I CAN'T CHAT LONG. I HAVE SOMETHING TO DO.

THAT'S FINE. I JUST WANT TO TELL YOU WHAT HAPPENED THE DAY I WENT TO THE PEABODY TO MEET YOU.

I couldn't believe how she wanted to play this clever game of how she had gone out to meet "Wayne" or "WhiteKnight" as far as she knew. I decided to entertain her for a minute or two more before I would log off and head to have a saucy night with my wife.

WHAT HAPPENED, BABE? I typed.

I RAN INTO AN EX.

My heart skipped a beat. I was almost afraid to ask, but I knew I had to.

EX WHAT? I responded.
EX-LOVER.
REALLY? SO, WHAT HAPPENED?
NOTHING.
NOTHING?
NO, NOTHING HAPPENED.
DID HE SPEAK?
NO. HE DIDN'T HAVE A CHANCE TO.
WHY NOT?
WELL, HE WAS HAVING LUNCH WITH A GORGEOUS WOMAN, AND I BELIEVE SHE WAS HIS WIFE.

This time my heart plummeted into my stomach. I felt an ache like no other. Surely, Karma couldn't be telling the truth. I decided to probe her more.

SO, YOUR EX IS MARRIED NOW?
YES.
WHY DIDN'T HE HAVE A CHANCE TO SPEAK?
OH, I DIDN'T WANT TO BE RUDE AND IMPOSE ON HIS LUNCH WITH HIS WIFE.
THAT WAS NICE OF YOU.
NO. WHAT WAS NICE OF ME WAS WHEN I PAID FOR THEIR LUNCH WITHOUT INTERRUPTING THEM AND THEN LEFT.

At that moment, Aisha appeared in the doorway, wearing nothing but her birthday suit.

"Are you going to join me or what?" she asked seductively.

It was a good thing she decided to surprise me with her nakedness because had she been fully clothed, she certainly wouldn't have understood the shock on my face as I stared at her. I couldn't speak. Karma's last comment confirmed what I thought I saw that day—her leaving the restaurant.

Karma questioned my pause.

HELLO? WAYNE, ARE YOU THERE?

I couldn't move. I couldn't think. I couldn't do anything. I glanced back at my beautiful wife and hoped she'd stay in the doorway.

DID YOU SEE MY LAST COMMENT? Karma questioned.

I closed the browser quickly then swallowed hard. Yes, I read her last comment. But instead of thinking about what was about to go down with my wife, I wanted to pinch myself hard to make sure I wasn't dreaming.

Karma

20

So, Nurse Mitchell wanted to play me, right? Well, I had news for her. I'd played them all before, and there wasn't a game known to mankind that she would beat me at. How dare she come at me with that little sympathetic act, pretending to care about how I was being treated by the good doctor. The bottom line was that she could potentially be a problem for me. Doc and I already had limited time to share. I refused to let her suspicions cause us more time restraints.

I had a plan—a master plan that was a surefire way of getting Nurse Mitchell out of my hair. When I learned Doc had taken off work, and our session had been cancelled, this gave me plenty of time to scheme. Besides, any time I knew he was on the premises, all I could do was think of ways to get to him. I made certain not to get into any trouble while he was off so he'd be proud of me once he got back. But poor Nurse Mitchell had no idea what I was cooking up for her.

On the way out onto the lawn, I stopped the unsuspecting woman before my escorting nurse and I reached the door. She was quite surprised when I pulled her aside and asked to speak with her.

"Yes, Jolley, is everything OK?" Nurse Mitchell asked as we stood alongside the wall.

I glanced at the nurse who was escorting me and the officer who stood nearby, giving them a raised eyebrow to let them know I needed privacy. They both nodded then slowly walked a few feet away. Satisfied that they shouldn't be able to hear us, I began.

"Everything is fine," I told her in a low tone. "I just wanted to know if we could have some time alone to talk. There're some things I think I should tell you."

I could see the interest heightening in her eyes as they widened. I shook my head and held my hand up for her to remain silent.

"Listen. I don't want to make any references to what I need to say in this hallway. We need to be some place no one can hear us."

"Well, why don't I just meet you on the lawn in half an hour? I just need time get another patient settled, and then I'll sign out for lunch. That way, no one will interrupt us."

I nodded, and then we started out the door. Once Nurse Mitchell saw where I would be sitting, she announced she'd join me shortly. I couldn't wait for the games to begin.

As I sat, scrolling through my iPod, Tee walked over and parked her little narrow behind.

"Hey, Karma," she said then giggled.

"Hey, Tee."

She sat staring at me for at least two minutes while I searched my iPod. I wanted so badly to keep ignoring her, but I couldn't. I learned a long time ago to be careful how I treated the hands that fed me. Tee was instrumental in helping me get on the outside of that ten-foot, concrete wall, and I was positive I would need her help again. After a few more minutes passed, I finally looked up then smiled.

"What's up, Tee? What's on your mind?"

"Oh, I was just wondering when you would notice something."

I shrugged. "Something like what?"

"Fee-Fee," she stated then giggled.

I shrugged again. "Okay, and what about her?"

"Can't you see? She isn't with me today."

I wanted to shrug again, but I played dumb and nodded. "Oh, yeah, I don't know what's wrong with me. Of course, I noticed she wasn't with you. I thought you meant something else. Where is she?"

"In our room. She was taking a nap, so I didn't want to disturb her. Besides, I thought you might miss our girl time. We haven't chatted or played cards in a while."

I was at a loss for words. Playing cards with Tee was the last thing on my mind. "Oh, well, um—"

"Karma, I see you have company," Nurse Mitchell interrupted.

I couldn't remember the last time I heard her call me by my first name. I frowned, in deep-thought as she stood over Tee and me.

"Oh, hi," Tee said.

"Hello, Teresa," Nurse Mitchell responded.

"I can go. I need to check on Fee-Fee anyway," Tee said, turning to leave.

"See ya later, Tee," I said, waving.

She waved over her shoulder. I could see jealousy all over her face before she left. That girl had a serious problem. Who gets jealous that the nurse came over to speak with me? I shook my head as Tee walked away. I'd have to make this interruption up to her though. I still needed to be in her good graces, so I could have more passes. Nurse Mitchell took a seat next to me.

"Fee-Fee?" Nurse Mitchell asked. "Who's Fee-Fee?"

"Felicia," I stated simply.

"Oh, her imaginary friend . . . so, she's given the friend another name now?"

"No, just a nickname."

"Wow." Nurse Mitchell shook her head.

"I know, right," was all I could say.

"So, Karma, is everything all right with you?"

I nodded. "Pretty much." I set my iPod in my lap then turned to her. "You know, Nurse Mitchell—"

"Darla," she said, cutting me off.

"Excuse me?"

"Darla. Call me Darla." She patted my knee.

Ooooohhh, so now this bitch wants to be friends. Now that she was sitting in front of me, obviously anxious to hear something juicy regarding the good doctor, she wanted to act like we were best girlfriends. I looked at the gleam in her eyes and the way her hands were clasped tightly and felt disgust. It was apparent that whatever news I could tell her would not remain our secret, but rather be used against my man. She had me twisted. I would never give her something to use against Doc. And just because she had that stupid-ass look in her eyes, I knew exactly what I needed to do. I continued to lead her on with my game.

"Okay, Darla. And you make sure to call me Karma, too. You know most times you call me Jolley."

"Oh, sure. No problem, Karma."

"Darla, listen. As I was about to say: I've been thinking. I don't know if I can have this chat with you here." I glanced around the place, giving her the notion that I was paranoid.

"What do you mean?"

"Darla, I don't trust anyone here, but you," I whispered. "I think this place is bugged, and I can't expose everything I need to say right here."

"Well, would you like to write it down?"

"Yes, if you don't mind," I responded.

To my amazement, "Darla," as she so wanted to be called, had a pen and a note pad in her uniform dress pocket. I should've known, given all the things she had to jot down while dealing with patients, but I was still surprised to see her so ready.

I took the items then began to scribble in an unknown handwriting. Oh, it was legible. I just didn't want the shit to look like I wrote it. My message read: MEET ME AT THE CORNER OF ELVIS PRESLEY BOULEVARD AND RAINES ROAD TOMORROW.

The look on Darla's face as she read the message was priceless. Although she had clearly read the note, she gave me a face filled with distorted muscles. She even squinted as though she couldn't see me clearly. She wrote me back. Her message read: HUH? WHAT DO YOU MEAN?

I responded, MEET ME AT THE WALGREENS THERE ON THE CORNER.

WAIT. I'M LOST. YOU CAN'T DO THAT, she wrote.

YES, I CAN.

Darla shook her head then wrote, HOW IS THAT POSSIBLE?

I CAN'T TELL YOU HOW. JUST MEET ME THERE TOMORROW AT 7 P.M. I'LL TELL YOU EVERYTHING YOU NEED TO KNOW ABOUT HIM.

Darla looked at me and slowly nodded, but I could see she was absolutely stunned at my request. I took all of the note paper from her then ripped them into as many little pieces as I could—just in case someone, namely Darla, was smart enough to put them back together. I wasn't too worried though. Not only would piecing the tiny specks of paper be next to impossible, but I had scribbled in a slant that would never be identifiable as mine.

I placed the micro bits inside Darla's dress pocket then patted it as if to say I knew our secret was safe. She would catch hell trying to rid her pocket of all the micro bits before washing that uniform dress, but that was totally her problem. As she stood to leave, Tee walked up.

"Okay, we're back," Tee said.

I knew exactly what she meant, so I played along with her delusional behind. "Hi, Fee-Fee. Did you enjoy your nap?"

Tee smiled. Darla still had a dumbfounded look on her face. This was a Kodak moment, but I didn't have a camera. Hell, I needed one. Who would believe me if I said I had Nurse, Darla Mitchell rendered speechless? Probably no one. Tee and I had some things to discuss, so I bid Darla good day.

"Well, Darla, I thank you for checking in with me. Everything is fine, and I know you're anxious to get home to your family, so I won't hold you."

"Um, sure. Thanks for the chat, Karma. I'll be chatting again with you soon."

She turned to leave, but not a moment too soon. I smiled at Tee then offered her and Fee-Fee to sit with me. By the next night, I would be Tee again, and she would be me. And Darla . . . well, let's just say, she'll only be herself, but a little more quiet.

Lawrence

21

*A*lthough I had taken off work, I didn't receive any calls from Karma. Aisha hadn't even received annoying calls during my time off. The next morning, I took off work again—still no drama from Karma. I wanted to call the hospital to question her behavior, but I decided not to for fear I would hear something I didn't want to know. I had a gala to attend that night, and I didn't want any news that would prevent me from having a great time.

It was still puzzling how Karma had managed to leave the hospital and return without anyone knowing. I knew I had to get to the bottom of the matter, but I couldn't let her know I knew she'd left the facility. Letting her know could mess up my opportunity to find out how she'd gotten away with it and who could've been helping her. Darla was way up high on my list of suspects. I was almost sure she'd been the culprit to help Karma all along. Time would tell. If I found out Darla was helping Karma plot against me, I would make Darla wish she'd never crossed me. She'd never be able to work in or around the greater Memphis area again.

I also needed to know why Karma sneaked out in the first place. It couldn't possibly have been to see the so-called WhiteKnight, or could it? But what worried me most was if she had followed me to the restaurant. If Karma knew how to find me outside of the psychiatric hospital, my troubles were bigger than I knew.

It was around 6:00 in the evening when Steve showed up dressed as if he was going to the Oscars. True, we were heading to a charity gala that would be benefiting True Hope Psychiatric Hospital, but I hadn't planned on wearing any of my thousand-dollar suits. He made me wonder if I needed to change when he called me on it.

"Dr. Lawrence Weisman, you've got to be kidding me!" Steve said, stepping inside the living room.

"What?" I responded.

"Please tell me you're going to do better than the James Bond Skyfall tux." He chuckled.

I gave myself a once-over and decided I looked fine. "Again I say—what?"

"Man, since when have you gone to a gala in your Macy's best? This is a red-carpet event."

"And I still don't see the problem here. This is a $250 tux."

Steve threw up his hands in an I-give-up fashion. "All right. Do *you*. But once you get there, just don't say I didn't try to warn you."

I glanced down at myself again and thought differently. The last event I'd attended was an awards banquet.

This one was going to be a high-profile, celebrity-style event. The media would be there. *Maybe I should wear something else,* I thought.

"Man, I can't stand you sometimes. I'm going to change," I told him.

"That's what's up!"

"Shut up and have a seat," I teased, heading toward the hallway that led to my bedroom. "The remote to the TV is somewhere on the couch."

As I entered the bedroom, I noticed Aisha sitting on the bed in her beige-colored body shaper that just about blended into her skin. She was reading something on the iPad in her lap. She should've been getting dressed before Steve's wife, Barbara, made it over. They had plans to ride together because Steve and I wanted to be at the gala early for the photo op with all the doctors and to mingle before the short program began. Aisha seemed startled as I spoke.

"Hey, babe," I said.

Aisha jumped and quickly flipped the cover to her iPad. "Oh, Larry, you scared me."

I paused at the foot of the bed, confused. "Really? So, what're you doing?"

"Nothing," she answered promptly. Aisha slid the iPad to the top-middle of the bed then got up and walked over to the mirror on the dresser. "So, I heard the doorbell ring. Was that Steve?"

"Yeah." I stared at her through the mirror. "Babe, what were you doing? Why did I startle you?"

She turned and faced me. "Oh, honey, it was nothing. I was just researching some more fertility options—you know, in case the pills don't help—that's all."

"Aisha, you jumped and slammed the cover closed."

She walked over to me then placed her hand on my chest. "Oh, I know. I think I was just startled because I didn't want you to know I was still looking for fertility options. You always seem so stressed when it comes to me talking about it."

I stared into my wife's eyes as she spoke. I could always tell when she was lying because she would bat her lashes and roll her eyes upward between every three words she spoke. *But what could she be hiding?* I wondered.

I turned slightly to look over my shoulder at the iPad on our bed. When I turned back to Aisha, she seemed nervous.

"What's wrong, honey?" she asked.

I looked into her eyes once again. The batting and eye-rolling had stopped.

"Nothing," I said. "You really need to get dressed."

"Oh, I am," she said, wandering into the closet.

I followed her to the closet then began to undress. Aisha questioned what I was doing. I explained the conversation Steve and I had then proceeded to change into my black Hart Schaffner Marx tuxedo. I knew exactly what shirt, tie, shoes and accessories that I'd wear with it. Surely, Steve would agree that with a $1400 ensemble, this tux was definitely designed for upscale, formal events. The satin lapels and four-button cuffs is what sold me before I ever tried it on.

After changing, I left the bedroom, leaving Aisha in the mirror, putting on makeup. I headed down the hall and into the living room. Steve had gotten pretty comfortable. His tuxedo jacket was on the back of the couch, and he sat, looking at TV with a drink in one hand and the remote in the other. I noticed my bottle of Crown Royal sitting on the coffee table.

"Dude, did I say help yourself to anything besides a seat on the couch and the TV remote?" I fussed.

Steve looked up at me then shrugged. He took a sip from his glass then answered, "I figured you wouldn't mind—seeing as how long it took you to primp." He took another sip then almost choked as he laughed.

"Primp? Please don't say that again. I'm a real man. I don't have a clue how to primp—*pimp*, maybe, but not primp."

The fact that Steve's laughter was nonstop and continued to get louder let me know he'd had more than the one drink I stood, watching him sip. It was clear I would be driving, without having said it.

I looked at the time on my phone. It was only 6:30. I hadn't planned to be at the gala, which would be held downtown at The Peabody Hotel, until around 7:30. Steve still had a ways to go before he downed that Crown, so I thought about checking my email to see if Karma had been reaching out.

"Hey, Steve, let me run into my office and check out something real quick. Don't pour another glass, man. I'll be ready to go in a few."

"Cool. I'll be right here, chillin' when you get back," he said, holding his glass up.

I shook my head then walked back to my office. I turned on the light then quickly logged into my personal email. Yes, Karma had reached out to me. There were a total of six emails, all with the current date, but they were grayed out as if I had already read them. This had me baffled. I hadn't been in my email account all day. As I slid the cursor to the first message, ready to open it, Aisha appeared in the doorway, wearing a thin-strapped, long sundress. I hurriedly clicked off my account.

"Aisha, you aren't wearing that, are you?" I took a second glance at the monitor to make sure my email was logged off.

"I'm not going," she responded. Her voice was shaken.

I glanced up, and that's when I noticed her dark, runny eyes. Her once-pretty face was ruined with mascara streaks and tears. I slowly stood to address her.

"Aisha, baby, what's wrong?"

"Ask Karma," she replied.

Nothing could've prepared me for her response. Even though I'd been in my email account and saw the grayed-out messages, I still hadn't thought Aisha was the one who read them.

"Aisha," was all I could say.

I had no clue what Karma had said in those messages, so I couldn't do much more than look at the pain on my wife's face. As I started toward her, she held out a halt hand, abruptly stopping me.

"Save it, Larry! You've been lying to me all this time and making me feel I'm the cause of this marriage falling to pieces!"

"Aisha, listen—"

"No, you listen, dammit! Your mental patient, Larry? Really? You're fucking your patient? And of all of your patients, you had to go and fuck the craziest one—the girl that has killed people, including her own mother and stepfather!"

"Aisha, I really can't believe you had the nerve to hack into my email account—"

"Well, believe it dammit! And I'm glad I did because you've lost your damn mind—screwing around with a mental patient—YOUR mental patient!"

I became irate as she continued to scream at me. I stepped closer to her as she stood just barely inside the room and began a little yelling tirade of my own.

"Well, how does it feel now that you've found what you were looking for?" I blurted to the top of my lungs. "Huh?" I was winded, but I continued. "I never meant for things to go this far, and I've been trying to get her out of my care, so I won't have to see her again. I know I was wrong, and I tried to hide it, Aisha! Hell, I never said I was perfect!"

"You don't have to be fuckin' perfect not to sleep with your patients, Larry, or not to mess around on your wife! You just need to have morals and standards, and more love for me than anything else in this world—like I do for you!"

"Okay, and so I did it! Now what?"

Aisha seemed taken aback by my question. She suddenly stopped crying and looked at me with disgust.

In a calm voice, she said, "I should tell on your ass myself—that's what."

She turned to walk away, but I spun her back around to face me. She put up a fight.

"Don't you put your damn hands on me," she said, swinging her fists with fast repetitions.

A couple of blows landed on my shoulders, but when the third one landed across my face, I shoved her into the closest wall, creating a lot of noise. Steve rushed in and pried my body from hers as I pressed her into the wall.

"C'mon, man, don't do this," he said, holding me back.

I was in such a fury, my chest heaved. "Not tonight, Aisha! Get your ass in that room and get dressed."

"Fuck you!" she screamed through tears. "I'm not going anywhere."

I tried to step around Steve, but he was stronger than I thought.

"Lawrence! Stop it, man! That's your wife!"

"Go back in the living room, Steve. Mind your business!"

"Well, hey, I tried not to get into y'all mess, but when I heard the physical stuff going on, I couldn't help it."

I poked my head around Steve and gave Aisha one final warning.

"Aisha, get dressed," I said calmly. "Barbara will be here in a minute." As I paused, she just looked at me.

"Steve and I are leaving now. I expect to see you at the gala in an hour. BE THERE," I roared.

Steve and Aisha both jumped when I belted, using all of my wind. I knew given all that Aisha might've learned from Karma's emails that she was in no partying mood. But I needed my wife by my side at the gala. All the other doctors would have their spouses, and it was only right that mine be there, too.

"Let's go," I told Steve then brushed by him.

Aisha jumped out of my way and into the hall as I got near her. She stood watching as Steve and I left. As we got into my car, Steve shook his head.

"You got something to say?" I asked.

"Your ass IS crazy. I only thought it before, but now I know for sure."

I didn't respond. Instead, I clicked the remote to let the garage door up then headed downtown. Steve and I didn't talk much on the way. He did let me know, however, that he didn't expect Aisha to show to the gala. I guess he was giving me time to wrap my brain around it so I wouldn't cut up with her once I got back home.

I needed a drink. Once at the gala, I couldn't wait for the photo op to be over so I could get some type of signature liquor in my system. I needed a mood-swinger in the worse way. Steve walked around and mingled, but I couldn't. Too many wild thoughts were taking over my mind. *How the hell did Aisha figure out the password to my account? Why was she snooping in the first place? What now?* The consequences that ran through my head nearly drove me crazy. I grabbed a drink from the open bar then sat at the first empty table I saw.

Steve and I were sitting at a table near the back since Aisha and Barbara hadn't shown up. We didn't know whether to expect them, but it was only proper to make sure we were seated where they could easily get to us and not disturb anyone since the program had started.

I kept looking toward the entrance for Aisha. Ten minutes into the program, I figured Steve must've been right—Aisha was not going to show. But neither had his wife.

I leaned in and whispered, "Hey, man, do me a favor and text Barbara. Find out where they are."

Steve sighed then pulled out his phone. As he began the text, Aisha slid into the seat next to me, and Barbara rounded the table to sit next to Steve. Barbara, didn't make eye contact with me, and neither did my wife. Aisha stared straight ahead. In spite the cold, stiff aura she gave off, she looked beautiful. I reached for her hand as she clutched her purse, but she wouldn't relent. So, I slid my arm around her shoulders instead.

"We're going to be okay," I whispered into her ear. She didn't blink, nor did she budge.

Ten minutes later, the program was over. People had begun to dance and mingle. Aisha and I sat at the table like strangers—not having anything to say. As I stared at her profile, something in my peripheral caught my attention. The woman with her back to me, chatting with a man near the door seemed familiar. She wore a black, open-back, laced dress—just like one I'd seen Aisha wear.

"Baby, look," I said, slightly nodding in the woman's direction. I didn't want anyone to see me pointing. "Don't you have a black dress like that one?"

Aisha turned to see what I meant. Just then, the woman turned her head slightly over her shoulder and caught a side-eye of me. I immediately popped out of my seat and almost pissed in my pants. The woman scurried out of there like Cinderella at midnight, leaving the man standing with a confused and what-was-that type of look on his face. I was just about to sprint after her when Aisha grabbed my arm.

"What's going on?" she asked.

I'd been waiting for my wife to say something to me since she got there, but when she finally did, I had no words for her. I just gave her a blank stare, hoping she wouldn't catch on to what had just happened.

Indeed the woman in the black dress was Karma. But what was more frightening was that I believed the dress came from my wife's closet.

Karma

22

---

*B*oy, oh, boy, was the look on my man's face priceless when he saw me at The Peabody Hotel! I laughed all the way out of that place. How dare he attend a gala and not invite me in the first place. I mean, sure he's married, but Doc is THE man. He could do anything he wanted. It would've been nothing for him to request a few hours of leave for me. Hell, those uppity people wouldn't have known who I was on his arm. I would've happily pretended to be Mrs. Weisman, considering that soon would be the plan anyway.

I was able to first, get to Doc's home, and then to the gala, courtesy of the late, nurse, Darla Mitchell. That's right. That bitch was no longer my problem, and her cute little, black Audi A5, two-door Coupe now belonged to me.

How dumb was Darla to actually follow through on my request to meet me outside the hospital? If I had been her, I would've asked more questions, and still declined to meet for fear of getting in trouble. Perhaps she didn't really believe I'd meet her. Oh, well! I showed her dumb-ass.

I hopped into Darla's car right where I told her to meet me—at the Walgreens on the corner of Elvis Presley Boulevard and Raines Road. Tee had an overnight pass that she let me use on the promise I'd bring her back some junk food. She wanted all the stuff we couldn't get inside True Hope like the Whatchamacallit candy bar, a box of Nerds, and a pack of Sour Straws. That girl had weird taste, but oh well. I just wanted the night out.

Josie came to sign me—Tee—out for the night. I wore a hoodie and placed one of Tee's small teddy bears up to my face so no one could get a good look. We got out of that place easily. She dropped me off at the Walgreens as I'd requested because she believed I had a boyfriend picking me up.

Once in Darla's car, I had to prompt her to pull off because she sat dumbfounded that I'd actually gotten out of the hospital and met her there.

"Um, we can go now," I told her.

"But how did you . . . who let—"

"Just go," I said. "I told you I can't tell you all of that. Let's go."

"Where to," she asked as she pulled off.

"Downtown. We need to find somewhere dark with no cameras or anything."

"Huh?"

"Well, I mean, I wouldn't want anyone finding out that I left the hospital, and then tracing my whereabouts back to you."

"Oh, ok. Yeah, you're right. I think I know a place."

Darla drove us downtown, and then parked in a dark secluded area near the Pyramid. I demanded we go for a walk out by the river, stating that I felt her car might've been bugged, and she complied. As we walked closer to the river, on top of uneven pavement that was covered by thousands of dark, ashy rocks, Darla began spilling her guts to me. I guess this was her effort to win my trust.

"And he just up and dumped me—for no reason," she said after having given details of the short-lived affair between her and Doc.

"But if he was attracted to you at first, then there had to be a reason he decided to stop seeing you."

Darla stared blankly at me. It was hard to see anything other than her eyes in the remote location we stood. I could imagine my eyes were mainly all she could see of me, too. She turned her back and took several steps forward. Her curvy figure became like a shadow in the distance. Shortly after she stopped walking, I heard her say something that seared my blood.

"I was pregnant with his child," Darla said with her back to me.

"Come again," I stated simply.

She wouldn't face me. "I was pregnant," she said louder. "He asked me to have an abortion, and I agreed." There was a brief pause. "But I didn't," she concluded.

"What? What was that?"

"I said, 'I didn't.' I didn't have the abortion. Our son is alive and well, but Lawrence isn't real sure of that. I only hinted to him recently that we have a child together." She finally turned to me. "You see, Karma, we have to stick together. I don't wish what happened to me on no one. That man could get you pregnant and leave you high-and-dry like he did me. You have to tell me what's been going on between you and Lawrence, so we can stop him from breaking other women's hearts."

This bitch was evil! She kept talking, apparently thinking her little sob story had made me want to turn on my man. I stared at her shaded silhouette in the night. Her shapeliness was a blur. She only looked like a thick blob to me at that point. I didn't hear much of what she continued to say. I only heard her previous words over and over in my head. The more I replayed her words, the more I was ready to make her pay for meddling in my business. When she didn't get a response from me right away, she stepped closer.

"Karma, did you hear me?"

"Huh? What?" I asked.

"I said what do you and Lawrence do in that office?"

"We fuck," I answered boldly.

I heard a slight gasp as she stepped closer. I looked down next to my foot and spotted a rock about the size of a honeydew melon. She took another step closer—close enough to look right into my eyes.

"What did you say?" she asked.

"You heard me. We fuck. I ride his dick, and he laps my fluent honey until he is full and can't take any more."

Darla didn't seem to know what to say. I chuckled a bit. The thought of the things that might've been going through her mind had me tickled. I had painted her a picture she probably never wanted to see. I chuckled again, and that must've made her not take me seriously.

"Karma, don't play with me," she snapped. "Are you telling me the truth?"

"Why would I have you meet me out here to spill you some lies?"

Darla began to pace. "All right then. Then I guess this means we've got to do something," she said walking back and forth. "I mean, we can't let him keep getting away with this."

I glanced at the large rock again. Darla continued to rattle on about how Doc thought he was invincible, and that he would have to pay for what he's done. It all began to sound like mush as a flash of me picking up the small boulder and smashing it over her head became real. And it *was* real. I stared at the rapid flowing blood. It ran from the top of Darla's head and down her face in three streams. Her eyes were dazed, as though she had no idea what just happened.

I raised the rock again and smashed it on top of her head harder. She fell to the ground with her eyes and mouth open. I kneeled and checked her pulse. There wasn't one. I searched her pockets for her keys and couldn't find them. I nearly panicked until I stood to move her body and heard them jingle under my feet. I picked up the keys and placed them in my pocket.

Darla had to be moved out of sight before daylight struck, so I drug her body to the edge of the small hill we were on, and then rolled her over, hoping to hear a loud splash. There was a splash all right, but it wasn't a loud one. It was too dark to see if her body sank, and I wasn't going down that hill to get a closer look. So, I just made my way back to her car and parked it at the Walgreens lot before calling Josie to pick me up to spend the night at her place.

The next day, I got up early to get on the computer. I checked into my eLovers Row account to see if WhiteKnight had contacted me, but he hadn't. I made up my mind to be done with that man. He was too full of games. I knew if he really wanted to meet me, he would've made it happen by now. Josie woke up and saw me on the computer.

"Hey, how did you get my password?" she asked.

"I didn't need it. You left your computer unlocked."

It was the truth. I didn't need any special skills to break into her computer. She might've been just as absent-minded as her sister and just plain forgot to secure it. I'm glad she made my job easy though. I was able to get all the information about where Doc lived along with the directions. All I needed then was to wait until that evening to make my move.

I sneaked out of Josie's house, which was in the Bartlett area, and then hitched a ride to the Whitehaven area so I could get back to my car from the Walgreens lot. I must say, that Audi A5 looked good as I approached it. I popped the lock, jumped in, and cranked it so I could load Doc's address into the navigation system.

I couldn't believe I was there in less than half an hour. I drove right pass the security booth because no one was inside, and the gate was even opened. As I eased down the street, looking for Doc's address, I witnessed a beautiful silver, convertible Jaguar pull into the huge driveway. I glanced at the address I'd written on a piece of note paper. *Yep, that's Doc's house alright.*

Doc's house looked bigger than I had seen on the Internet. I had no idea who was in that car, but I had every intention to find out. I parked just down the street and watched a classy, big-boned lady step out, wearing a yellow, floor-length, A-line, one-shoulder, chiffon dress. The waistline was tapered with what looked like hundreds of tiny, glistening rhinestones. The sista was sharp!

As the woman made her way to the front door, it opened, and the same beautiful woman I'd seen at TGI Fridays with Doc appeared. Once the visitor was inside, the door closed. I got out of my car. What I would do next, I really didn't know. I didn't have a plan. I just knew I wanted to get inside. I thought about walking up to the door and ringing the doorbell, but what would I do next? I couldn't pretend to be a salesperson. I had nothing to sell.

I stepped in front of the door anyway. A voice in my head told me to try to open the door. This was a rich neighborhood. Based on what I'd seen on TV, people were comfortable in such elite neighborhoods and often didn't lock their doors, especially in the daytime. It was evening, but the sun hadn't fully set.

I turned the knob, and the door cracked. I eased it open some more then peeped inside. I didn't see or hear anyone, so I made my way in and closed the door. That's when I heard a chirping sound from the alarm, signaling movement at the door. I paused, waiting to hear someone heading in my direction, but after nearly a minute passed, I figured no one would come.

The living room was straight luxury like I'd never seen. My man had class. He had to have paid at least thirty or forty grand on living room furniture alone. I heard a voice coming from what looked like a hallway, so I ducked on the other side of the couch.

"No, just set it on the bed. I'll be right back once I check the front door," the woman said.

I peeped and discovered Doc's wife, locking the front door. Then, the other woman yelled from the back.

"Was it locked?" she asked.

"No," Doc's wife yelled. "But it is now."

The other woman's voice got closer. "You know, after everything you've been through today, Aisha, I say we need a drink."

Aisha? I thought. *So, that's her name.*

"You know, Barbara, you're right. I'm going to need a drink if I'm going to make myself go to that damn gala with him. It would only be for appearances because after finding out all the shit he's been doing, this marriage is over. I care nothing about being seen with him at The Peabody tonight."

Over? I smiled inside. *Yes!*

"Now, sweetie, you don't mean that," her friend said.

"Yes, I do, Barbara. Can you imagine your husband messing around on you? And with one of his patients?"

"One of his patients?" Barbara yelled.

"Yes, and you'll never believe which one," Aisha told her.

"Who?" Barbara's tone was strained. "Oh, I don't know if I even want to know. He could be in a whole lot of trouble, Aisha."

"You remember the woman on the news over a year ago—the crazy one that—"

"Oh, Aisha, please don't tell me. The fact that you even know any of her business violates the laws."

Crazy? I thought.

"I don't know her business," Aisha continued. "I only know what's been on the news, but I've been violated, too! She screwed my husband, and God only knows how many times," Aisha said, sounding as if she was about to burst into tears.

"Aisha, let's get that drink, honey, and then we can chat some more about this. As twisted as this situation is, I'm just not ready to see you and Lawrence split up."

"What would you do, Barbara? Huh?"

There was a brief pause, and then Barbara responded, "I don't know what I'd do."

"Well, thank you for at least admitting that," Aisha said. "C'mon. I have some Moët, chilling in the kitchen."

I heard their voices fade as they left the room. When I felt comfortable they wouldn't see me, I tipped down the hall to the last bedroom. It was the only one with a light on. I could tell by the many dresses scattered on the bed that this bedroom was where Doc and Aisha slept. I took a look around, admiring the place I'd soon be laying my head. When I heard the two women's voices coming up the hall, I eased into the walk-in closet and hid behind her long, evening gowns.

"So, what made you hack into the man's email, Aisha?" I heard Barbara ask.

"You know, Barb, I think I just had that woman's intuition. I mean, something didn't feel right between us."

"And what did this woman say in the messages?"

"Oh, she went on and on about how much she loved him and all the things he does to her in his office—too explicit for me to even mention, by the way—AND that she has a plan that would help them finally be together—as man and wife!"

"Man and wife? Does she even know he's married?"

"I have no idea, Barbara. He wears his ring, but we didn't get to discuss that before he put his hands on me."

"Aisha, no! Tell me he didn't!"

Put his hands on her? That doesn't even sound like my man. I smiled inside and thought, *Oh, I guess he really does love me. He put his hands on her because he was defending me during their argument. That's what the bitch gets! She should've stayed out of his email.*

Aisha must've chosen one of the dresses on her bed because as I peeked at her through the many gowns, I saw that she was dressed, and she grabbed a pair of Christian Louboutin shoes when she entered the closet. That was the first time I'd ever laid eyes on a pair in real life. I only knew the designer because I read the name on the box she got them out of.

It didn't take her and Barbara long to get out of there. I eased into the hallway to see if I could hear their voices. The only thing I heard was the rapid chirping sound of the alarm being set, and then a long beep that signaled it was set. I knew that would make it hard for me to get out of the house without incident, so I had to think fast.

I went back into the closet and grabbed a few things I figured I could use—one being a sexy, black dress and heels I could wear to the gala. I even went into the bathroom closet and found a pillow case I could use to stash my new items. On the way out, I spotted her CHI flat irons on the bathroom counter. I swiped those, too, because they would come in handy.

By the time I was on my way out of the house, I figured Aisha and her friend should be long gone. Once I hit the corner into the living room, the alarm blared. It startled me at first, but then I knew I just needed to get the hell out of there. I opened the front door and darted out as quickly as I could. I made it down the street and to my car without a problem, but as I was about to pull off, I saw Barbara in that shiny Jaguar with Aisha on the passenger side, riding pass me. I slid down in my seat a bit then watched as Aisha and Barbara went inside the house.

It was time to roll. I cranked the car then drove as far away from that area as possible before pulling over to enhance my beauty. I had a gala to attend, and then it would be back to Josie's crib to hear her mouth about me sneaking out. I could only hope she would be mad and then get over it, because I wasn't quite ready to commit another murder. I had slated Murder Number Two for Aisha, but sequence was of no importance. I just needed to get the job done, so I could finally be Mrs. Lawrence Weisman.

Lawrence

23

We were all out of breath by the time we stumbled into my home through the entrance from the garage. I didn't even let the garage door down in my haste to get inside to check out my home. Aisha and Barbara jetted down the hallway, heading to my bedroom. I turned off the alarm as Steve yelled that he was heading to check out my guest rooms upstairs and the home theater.

After searching my office, I checked my den, the laundry room, and the formal dining area. Nothing seemed out of place. I rushed to the bedroom where Aisha and Barbara had ransacked our closet.

"Is this it?" I heard Barbara ask.

"No," Aisha answered. "It's lace, knee-length with a high neck, and the back is open."

"I'll take over from here, Barbara," I said. "I know exactly what it looks like."

As Barbara stepped out of the closet, Steve came into the room. "Everything looks to be okay, Lawrence," he said.

"You look in the bathrooms, too?" I asked, yelling from the closet as I fumbled through dresses.

"Yeah. It appears no one has been here."

"Look, why don't we all just take a deep breath," Barbara said. "I'm sure if we just call True Hope and verify this woman is in her room, we'll all feel much better."

Aisha sprinted from the closet. "No, I've got something better—I'm calling the police."

I dropped the dress in my hand then ran over to stop her. Steve was just on my tail. We both grabbed phone from Aisha at the same time. Steve snatched it from me.

"No police, Aisha," Steve said.

"And why not?" she yelled. "This is my life in jeopardy. This woman has already been proven crazy, not to mention she's a murderer. I'm in fear for my life!"

"But, Aisha, calling the police could get me and Lawrence in trouble," Steve responded.

"Well, can somebody at least call and have the hospital check on her?" Aisha asked.

"I was just about to do that," I said, reaching for the phone, but Steve wouldn't hand it to me.

"Man, you're not thinking. If you call to check on her, and she's not there, you'll trigger all kinds of suspicions and investigations your way. Don't you think they'll want to know how you knew to check on her?"

"Because he saw her ass at the gala!" Aisha yelled. "Give me my phone, Steve, or else I'll just use my cell."

"Aisha, stop just one minute," I yelled. "Let's just try to figure some things out first."

"Like what, Larry?" she snapped. "There's a maniac on the loose from the hospital, and I'm pretty sure this is *not* her first time getting out!"

"Aisha, I promise you we'll get on top of it as soon as we get back to work," Steve said. "We're well aware of the things this woman has been doing. Lawrence and I are working on getting her to another facility, so he won't have to deal with her anymore."

"Okay, but in the meanwhile, I'm just supposed to let her come into my home and wreak havoc?"

"Aisha, I said the woman *looked* like her," I stated firmly. "We don't know for sure if that was her at the gala, and so far it appears she was never here."

"Okay, but where's the dress, Larry?" Aisha asked plainly.

We both darted back into the closet to look some more. That black dress had to be there. One of us needed to find it. Barbara yelled to us as we searched.

"Aisha, are you sure you might've left the door cracked, which could've set off the alarm just as we headed down the street?"

"Yeah," Aisha yelled back. "I've done it before. But then again, that maniac had to have come here. She must've triggered the alarm as she left. That must've been how the door was left opened!"

As Aisha and I searched the closet, I heard Steve and Barbara arguing about what a big mess this situation was. I didn't have a rebuttal. They were absolutely right. I had no business crossing the lines with Karma, and now my life had become a living hell. If only I could reverse the first time I let her seduce me, my life would've remained normal.

I heard Aisha panting as she fanned through the many dresses on her end of the closet. I looked up to see tears flowing down the side of her cheek like there would be no end to them. I wanted to say something to soothe her—make her know that I was sorry, but I couldn't think of much more to say than the words "I love you," which she probably wouldn't believe.

I walked the short stretch in the closet to reach her, and then I raised my hand to wipe her tears. She slapped my hand down before I could touch her. Just then, Barbara called out to us again.

"Lawrence, did you let down the garage and reset the alarm?" Barbara asked.

I turned and quickly left the closet. "Um, no—oh, I mean, I don't know. Why?"

She and Steve looked at each other. "Nothing," Steve said. "We just thought we heard something, but maybe we're just a little paranoid."

Aisha appeared from the closet and stood next to me. "What's wrong? What's going on?"

"Nothing, Aisha," Barbara responded. "So where's the dress?"

Aisha and I looked at each other for a second or two then we both turned to her and said. "It's not here."

Just then, Steve raised his hand and said, "Sshh. Did anybody else hear that?"

"Hear what?" I asked.

"I think somebody's in the house, man," Steve said softly.

"What?" I yelled.

"Yeah, I just heard it, too," Barbara seconded.

We all got silent for a few seconds, and then a loud crash flowed through the hallway from the living room. Everyone jumped, but Steve and I bolted down the hallway toward the living room.

"Y'all stay here," Steve yelled to our wives as we ran.

Though unarmed, Steve and I approached the living room ready for battle. No one seemed to be in there, but somehow, my four-hundred-dollar, 18x24, Christofle wedding frame was no longer over the fireplace. It was smashed on the hardwood floor. I looked around the living room again for signs of someone having been there.

"I'm going to check the garage." Steve brushed pass me.

"A'ight."

I bent down to look at the broken pieces to the frame that once housed the picture that captured one of the happiest days of my life. I glanced above the mantle over the fireplace, wondering if the frame had somehow fallen on its own. Then, my thoughts were interrupted by the panic-stricken howls of Steve.

"Lawrence! Hey, Lawrence, c'mere! Hurry! C'mere!" he yelled from the garage.

I scrambled from the floor, into the kitchen, and out the door that led to the garage. I stumbled upon Steve as he leaned on my car, holding his arm.

"What happened?" I asked, out of breath.

"It was her. Karma was here."

I ran toward the entryway of the garage and saw a small black car speeding away. It was too dark to tell what type of car it was, and the driver sped away like a criminal racing from a crime scene. That made it extremely difficult for me to determine any details. I turned back to Steve.

"Steve, are you okay?"

"Ah, yeah," he answered, wincing. "She hit me across the arm with that tire iron." He pointed to the object that lay tilted against the wall as it had been tossed in the corner. "I couldn't hold her."

"Damn, Steve, I'm sorry. I sure didn't mean for you to get hurt."

"Don't worry about. I don't think my arm is broken. I'll live."

"But, damn, though. Shit just got real. This bitch is breaking out of the hospital and showing up at my house now."

"This is fucked up, Lawrence. I want to help you, man, but I can't be caught up in this bullshit. I have a wife and family who depend on me. My whole livelihood will be at stake if I get twisted in this mess."

"I understand. I can't ask you to help me any further. I've got to dig myself out of this grave on my own."

"What are you going to tell Aisha about what happened?"

"Nothing. Can you straighten that arm up?"

"I'll try."

"C'mon inside and have a seat," I told him as I pressed the button on the wall to close the garage door.

I had my mind made up not to tell our wives the truth about Karma having been there. I even developed a quick story in my head about how the neighbor's cat had gotten in and climbed the mantle, causing the wedding frame to fall. However, I had to come to grips with the truth sooner than I thought. Barbara and Aisha met us face-to-face as we entered the kitchen.

"She was here, wasn't she?" Aisha demanded to know.

I was about to tell a lie when Barbara noticed Steve couldn't straighten up his arm.

"What happened out there?" Barbara asked him. "What's wrong with your arm?"

"Oh, nothing, babe. I'll be okay," he said.

Barbara reached to touch Steve, and he winced in pain. "Oh, no, honey, you may need to go see a doctor."

Aisha gasped then ran toward the cordless phone, sitting on the counter.

"Aisha, what're you doing?" Barbara asked.

"I'm calling the police!" she screamed.

I started toward her, but Steve beat me over there and addressed Aisha with a softer approach than I had in mind.

"Aisha, listen. I know you're scared, but I really need you to put down the phone and listen to me," he said.

"Steve, that woman is dangerous—not to mention she's not supposed to be away from the mental facility anyway! Hello! Did anybody forget that she's an escapee?"

"No, no, Aisha," Steve said calmly. "We're well aware of the situation and how dangerous she can be. But, listen. Although she has mental issues, Karma is very smart. She won't be back here. In fact, I'm willing to bet she's on her way back to sneak into the hospital right now."

"What's the deal, Steve?" Aisha asked. "Why're you taking up for this woman and Lawrence? Huh? Were you fucking her, too?"

Barbara interjected. "Now wait just a minute!"

"No, you wait, Barbara," Aisha said. "Let him answer."

And Steve answered, "Hell naw! The nerve of you insinuating I'm indecent! Your man might be my friend, but you better be glad he's got somebody like me on his side to help him understand when he's wrong. I'm only trying to save his reputation, and oh yeah, your marriage, too—that is, if you still want it. Besides, if my name gets dragged into this shit, I'm sending y'all through the ringer. I will *not* lose my career over this!"

"Aisha, I can't believe you!" Barbara said. "Let's go, Steve!"

Clearly angry, Barbara pulled her husband's arm, causing him to wince. Steve straightened up then followed Barbara into the living room and to the front door. Aisha and I followed them and watched as they left. She turned to me and fussed some more.

"Look what you've caused!" She stared me in the eyes. "And you think I'm going to stay here with you? I love you, Larry, but I will never forgive you for this!"

Aisha stormed toward our bedroom. I made sure the doors were locked then reset our alarm. I'd heard the saying, "In too deep," but now I knew the exact meaning of it. The more I tried to toss the dirt off my back, the more it felt like it was piling on, burying me in a bottomless grave.

I still needed help, but if Steve wasn't going to help me? Who would? As I walked toward the bedroom, preparing for more arguments with Aisha, it dawned on me who I could get on my side. Colby Patterson.

Karma

24

What a freakin' weekend! I thought as I sat in the library Monday close to noon, logging into my eLovers Row account. First, I happily made Nurse, Darla Mitchell a memory of the past. I must admit, killing her was so easy, I almost regretted not having a challenge, or at least having her put up a fight. Anyway, what was done was done.

The hospital was pretty quiet, and everything seemed normal, so I could only imagine Darla's absence hadn't been discovered. Even if her body managed to sink into the river that night, I knew it wouldn't be long before it surfaced again. The Mississippi River, as most rivers do, would rise and fall depending on the rain and other weather.

Next on my list of Possible Kills In A Weekend was that I almost had to take out Dr. Steven M. Johnson. What a wuss he was! He couldn't even scratch like a girl if he wanted to. When he saw me coming with that tire iron, he looked as if he didn't know whether to run or fight. He elected to swim, I think. At least that's what it looked like as he dropped his head and rapidly tossed his arms forward. I paused just short of his flailing fists and waited for him to realize he hadn't landed a blow. He stopped and looked up at me. I raised the tire iron and came down with a mighty blow. He had blocked his head with his forearm. Before I could land another blow, he began screaming out like a girl—calling for Doc. I went ahead and got out of there.

I had a mind to hurt Josie—just to shut her mouth about me having sneaked away from her, but I didn't kill her because I figured I might need her again. She ranted about how much trouble she might be in because of how late we were returning to the hospital. I nodded, gave her a few "Yes, ma'am," responses, and even apologized a few times. She was still pretty angry, but she put on a straight face once we returned to True Hope. She gave the sign-in clerk an excuse about car trouble and that we couldn't call because her phone had died. She was given a written warning and one was also placed in Tee's file. She rolled her eyes at me before turning to leave the facility. The nighttime escort nurse and security officer led me to Tee's room and locked me in. I had to sleep there all night before Tee and I could exchange rooms the next day.

I sort of missed chatting with Wayne. He had just sort of disappeared. I wanted to at least chat one more time with him—maybe get some closure on why he'd up and stop chatting with me. Perhaps he found out about me—who I really was and all I'd done to land myself in True Hope. Oh, well, and there I was waiting patiently for him

to pop up online. He didn't, so in my boredom, I decided
to get into some other mischief. There were some important emails I needed to send, and it would make all the
difference in the world regarding my upcoming wedding.

"There . . . that oughta get it," I said aloud as I
pressed the SCHEDULE tab in my email.

I made sure that the appropriate recipients would
receive them at the appointed time. No one was in the
computer room with me, but even if they were, talking to
myself wouldn't have mattered. Almost everyone in our
nuthouse did. As I sat back in my chair, my mind began to
wonder to Doc. I knew he'd seen me at that gala, and I was
sure he even knew I had shown up at his home a couple of
times—so why hadn't he reached out to me? Did he even
care? He told me once before that he did. I couldn't understand why my actions over the weekend hadn't warranted
his attention. I couldn't take the silence anymore. I quietly
left the computer room, sneaked my way pass the library
Grinch, sitting at her station, and then headed down the
hall toward Doc's office.

The staff at True Hope was slipping. No one seemed
to notice me wandering the halls toward the psychiatrists'
offices on my own. Security seemed too busy, and even
many of the nurses looked distracted by something on the
computers at their stations. I walked right by them as if I
was well within my rights, and since no one gave me hell
about it, I kept it moving.

Once I made it to Doc's office, I turned to see if
anyone was watching—the coast was clear. I eased open
the door, and to my surprise, he wasn't in there. I closed

the door behind me then headed around his desk to have a seat. His computer was still up, which let me know he must've left only moments before I made it there.

"Hmm," I said aloud. "I wonder what the good doctor has been up to lately."

I toggled to another browser he'd left open, and to my surprise, I saw the heading to eLovers Row. *What the hell?* I thought. I skimmed the site further and noticed his log in name—WhiteKnight. *WhiteKnight?* I was livid! Doc had been playin' me all along. The infamous WhiteKnight had been Doc all this time, and that explained why the sudden disconnect of exchanges. He must've figured out in my messages that I'd been sneaking out of the hospital.

As I began to think of all the things I wanted to do to get back at Doc for playing with my emotions, I heard the toilet flush in his office restroom. I quickly got underneath the desk. I had a million thoughts run through my head, one of them being to just face him head on when he got out of the restroom.

I heard the sink shut off and the cranking of his paper towel dispenser, and then the squeaking of his restroom door opening. He cleared his throat, and it sounded as if his footsteps were headed in my direction, but he was interrupted by a knock on the door.

"Hey, Lawrence, you ready to go, man?" I heard Dr. Johnson say.

"Naw, Steve, I think you'll have to go to lunch without me."

"Why? What's up? Working on something?"

"Naw, man. It's my stomach," Doc replied. "I told you I haven't been right since the other night. Knowing that girl can get to my house got my stomach in knots. I can't keep anything down."

"Yeah, I can imagine. And I come bearing more bad news."

"Aw, shit. Steve, I don't know if I can take any more bad news. Do I need to sit down?"

"Yeah, bro'. I think you might."

I heard Doc take an exasperated breath. "Look. Just hit me with it."

"Word around the office is Darla's missing."

"What do you mean 'missing,' Steve? She didn't report to work today?"

"No, she didn't come in today, and nobody has seen her since last Thursday when she got off."

"Thursday! She's been missing since Thursday?" Doc said, clearly sounding upset. "Has anybody notified the police?"

"Yeah, from what I've heard, her parents made the report and detectives are all over it."

"Wow . . . just fuckin' wow! I can't believe this shit!"

"Lawrence, are you thinking what I'm thinking?" Dr. Johnson asked.

"Yeah, *that bitch* had something to do with Darla's disappearance."

That did it. I couldn't stay hidden any longer. I popped from under the desk and stood firm.

"Well, say what you wish, but *'that bitch'* is right here, and let's see if you can prove I had something to do with her disappearance."

Doc's face went pale. "Karma, what the fuck are you doing here? I ordered your ass on 24/7 lock down."

I laughed. "Oh, yeah. Well, take it up with your staff. Everybody has been slipping today." I giggled as I approached him. "I mean, nobody has been doing their job around here."

Doc nearly growled at me. "Look, I'm getting ready to call security to come get your ass! And I'm reporting you for leaving this building. Who's been helping you anyway? Darla?"

"Helping me? I don't do *compadres*, sidekicks, or partnerships. I work alone."

"Just call security, Lawrence," Dr. Johnson said.

"G'head. I ain't scared. I was only in here because the good doctor asked to see me," I responded.

"What?" they both said in unison.

"In other words, Doc, it's your word against mine."

"You know, Karma, I could really hurt you right now," Doc said.

"Oh, yeah, well the feeling is mutual." I pointed at Doc. "How dare you play with my emotions! Why did you create WhiteKnight?"

He looked stunned for a second, glanced at his computer, and then answered, "To keep up with what your conniving ass was thinking and doing."

"I-DON'T-LIKE-PEOPLE-MESSING-WITH-MY-EMOTIONS!"

"Calm down, Karma," Dr. Johnson said, grabbing my arm.

I jerked from him. "This ain't what you want! Did you not get enough the other night?"

"I can't believe you brought your ass to my house," Doc screamed.

"Well, believe it, baby, because it's soon to be *our* house. It's just a matter of time now when I officially become Mrs. Lawrence Weisman."

"Karma, Lawrence is happily married already," Dr. Johnson said.

"Not if Aisha mysteriously comes up missing," I said boldly.

Lawrence lunged at my throat, and we fell onto the couch as he proceeded to choke the life out of me. First, I saw stars, and then everything started to go black. I must've only been out for a few seconds because when I awoke, I saw Dr. Johnson struggling to keep Doc away from me.

"Lawrence, man, this is not the way," he said.

"*Please* let me at that bitch."

"Listen, man. We've got to do things the right way. C'mon now. Get yourself together."

I was a bit woozy as I stood. "Wow, baby, I didn't know you had that in you. Good for you—my man's a fighter when he has to be."

"Fuck you, Karma!" Doc spat.

"Yeah, yeah," I said, turning to leave. "Well, baby, I forgive you this time—seeing as how we have a wedding coming up soon. Oh, and Dr. Johnson, you're not invited. Doc and I have to do this alone."

"Karma, get back to your room, and don't come out," Dr. Johnson said, holding on to Doc's arms. "We're going to notify security to keep a tight rein on you."

I laughed as I opened the door. "Good luck."

I left Doc's office, softly singing "Here Comes the Bride" as I sashayed down the hall.

Lawrence

25

I was mortified. Darla's parents told the hospital's director the last time anyone had heard from her was last Thursday night. Apparently, she mentioned to one of her friends that she had an important meeting with someone, but she didn't mention who or where. My stomach was still in knots because I was almost sure Karma had something to do with Darla's disappearance.

I paced the length of my office once Steve left. I made sure to call to the nursing staff and security first though. I asked why they hadn't honored my order to keep Karma in her room all day. No one had an explanation, but they offered apologies and promised to get on it. If I could only tell them the real truth—that Karma had been somehow leaving the premises and could possibly be responsible for Darla's disappearance. They'd know the severity of my order then.

Darla, I thought. *I still have her number.* I scrambled to the phone, so I could try to call her myself. Perhaps she was just taking a much-needed break from the rest of the world, but I had to see if she would answer if she saw that it was me.

"C'mon, c'mon, c'mon," I said aloud as the first ring sang loudly through my office. I had set the speaker.

The second ring didn't fully go through before I heard her voice.

"Well, well, well. Look who's finally calling me," she said. "It's about time! But guess what—I'm not available, so please leave a message at the tone." She gave a slight giggle then I heard the beep.

Darn it! Bad timing, Darla, I thought.

"Darla, where are you? This is Lawrence. Everyone is worried sick about you. Please give me a call when you get this message. I need to know you're okay. Call me."

I hung up and started back in front of my desk to continue pacing, but my desk phone rang back almost immediately, stopping my haste. I snatched it off the hook and answered.

"True Hope Psychiatric. Dr. Weisman speaking. How may I help you?"

"Oh, yes, Dr. Weisman, I hope I didn't disturb you. This is Colby Patterson, and I'm returning your call."

I took a deep breath. I was relieved that he actually returned my call, but I was also dismayed that it hadn't been Darla calling me back. I wasn't sure what I needed to say to the man, but I knew I needed his help in the worse way. I swallowed hard then spoke.

"Um, yes, Mr. Patterson. First, let me thank you for returning my call. I really need to meet with you, if at all possible. There's a pressing matter at hand, and it should be discussed privately."

"Is this about Karma Jolley, Dr. Weisman? I understand she's been in your care for a little over a year now."

"Um, yes. The matter does deal with Ms. Jolley. Are you willing to meet with me, so we can have a discussion?"

He was silent. Too quiet. I almost wanted to call his name—just to make sure he was still on the phone. Just when I was about to speak up, he asked, "Has this woman escaped your facility? I mean, my wife and I were just beginning to feel secure again."

"No, Mr. Patterson, Ms. Jolley is still housed in our facility, but I really do need your help with something."

"Okay, so should I meet you at your office?"

"No, sir. If you'll meet me at The Capital Grille on Poplar Avenue, that will be great. Dinner and drinks are on me?"

"Hmm. This is a strange request, Dr. Weisman, but I'm curious to know what's going on. I'll meet you there, say around 7:30?"

"Great. Thanks, Mr. Patterson. I look forward to meeting you."

I hung up the phone then called Aisha to explain my plan and what I wanted with Colby Patterson. Aisha was still very angry with me—not talking much, and when she did, it was in regard to moving out and divorcing me. I wanted to save our marriage, but of course, I would. I was the cheater and the one had created a large whole in our union. I wasn't sure Aisha would ever forgive me, but I had to keep trying.

I went home, showered and changed into jeans and a dark blue polo shirt. If I would have put on slacks and dress shoes, Aisha might've sworn I wasn't really going to meet Colby Patterson, but instead, meet with another woman. She hardly even looked at me, let alone spoke to me. I noticed that the dresser was free of her items and even some of her clothes were missing from the closet. I wanted to question her, but I didn't have time for the argument. I needed to meet with Mr. Patterson, and then hopefully come back home to my wife still waiting for me.

I pulled my BMW Z4 up to the valet for parking. I'd been to this place a few times before, twice with Aisha, and once with Steve and a few other colleagues. I knew that with it being Monday night, chances of a huge crowd would be slim. I was right. As I approached the door, I was able to walk right in and give the hostess my reservation info. She advised me that my party was already seated and waiting for me, and then I was led to the table.

I was surprised to see a couple sitting at the table when I got there. The man stood and introduced himself.

"Dr. Weisman," he said, stretching his hand for me to shake it. "I'm Colby Patterson, and this is my wife, Audrie."

I nodded as I shook his hand. "Nice to meet you both," I responded. I also reached to shake Mrs. Patterson's hand.

They were a nice looking couple. I could only wonder how they felt now that they're lives were Karma-free. Colby was pretty much as I'd pictured him. He might've been a couple of years or so younger than me, but he and I were about the same height and complexion. He also bore no signs of aging as I did with the tinge of gray hair in my goatee. As I slid into my seat, he went on to explain his wife's presence.

"I know you're surprised to see my wife here, but when I told her where and what I was doing, she insisted on coming," he said. "I can never say no to the Missus." He chuckled a bit then kissed her on the cheek.

"Oh, okay. Not a problem," I lied.

I really had only planned on having a man-to-man talk, but now that his wife was present, I had to rethink what I would say to him.

"And I'm paying for my wife and myself—"

"No, no . . . you're my guest—both of you. I'm taking care of the bill."

He smiled then glanced at his wife, seemingly for approval. She nodded and smiled also.

"Alright, Dr. Weisman, if you insist," she said.

"I do. And thank you for accepting."

Our waitress came over and took drink orders before we could begin any discussion. I ordered the Classic Manhattan, which was made of my main ingredient, Gentleman Jack and garnished with sour cherries. The Pattersons both ordered the Adults Only Arnold Palmer, made up of vodka, tea and lemonade.

After a few sips of our drinks, I knew I needed to get right down to it. "So, I know you two are wondering why we're here." They stared at me intently. "So, listen. I've asked to meet with you, Mr. Patterson, because I'm at a loss with Karma. She's out of control, and I really would like to know from you how you regained your peace."

"She was captured—that's how," he said bluntly.

"Well, I know that," I responded. "I mean, I guess what I'm trying to say is before her captivity—what did you do to stay on top of her games?"

"Dr. Weisman," Mrs. Patterson said, "Let me ask you this straight up. "Is Karma a threat right now to anyone—my husband, myself, our family—you?"

I swallowed real hard. I picked up my glass to take a sip, but my nerves caused me to spill a little over the top of my hand. I set the glass down then used a napkin to wipe my hand. I knew I needed to tell them the truth. But I also knew I couldn't come clean about everything. I picked up my glass again, but this time her husband spoke up.

"Dr. Weisman—" he started.

"Lawrence. You can call me Lawrence for the sake of this meeting."

They looked at each other then back at me. "Okay, Lawrence. Call me Colby. Listen is there something I need to know?"

"Yes, Colby," I responded. "I know I made you believe earlier that everything was fine with Karma's housing situation, but the truth is," I said then cleared my throat. "The truth is somehow she's been able to leave the facility when she wants without anyone noticing."

"What!" they both exclaimed.

"Wait. Hear me out. We're working to rectify the situation. She's been put on 24/7 lockdown for now, so you don't have to worry about anything."

"If there's nothing to worry about, why are we here?" Mrs. Patterson asked.

"I'm getting to that," I answered.

The waitress returned to take our orders. Truth be told, my stomach was still in knots, and I was afraid to order anything. But since I hadn't eaten much all day, and I was now drinking, I knew I needed to put something in my stomach. I ordered several different appetizers for us to sample, and once they placed their dinner orders, I requested the glazed salmon as my meal. I figured I'd start with the appetizers and a salad, and if I couldn't get to the salmon, I could take it home to Aisha.

We continued to talk over dinner. I had requested Colby help me catch Karma outside the facility by luring her to a particular place. Once she could be discovered outside the facility, she would either automatically be transferred or sent into the general prison population. I wanted to declare her sane enough for prison. Karma would be more disciplined there, plus she'd be farther away from Memphis than the True Hope facility, which was only just up the road in Atoka, Tennessee—not even thirty miles. Mrs. Patterson still had concerns.

"But I thought you said she's on lockdown," she said.

"True, but I'm the one who ordered it," I said. "I can order it lifted on the day she thinks she's going to meet Colby face-to-face."

"Why should we help you? Is there not another way to catch her out of order?" Mrs. Patterson said.

I was becoming frustrated with this lady. This is why I had only wanted Colby to come. Just like all the women I know in my life, his wife asked too many damned questions. Had it just been Colby and me, the discussion would've probably been over. He would have agreed to the plan, and everything would've been set in motion long before now. But I had to endure her.

"Mrs. Patterson, I assure you I've thought of everything. It's not just about helping me. It's about protecting everyone. Karma has a lot of sense. She's still in the mind, though, that she can do whatever she wants and have whatever she wants. She needs to be in prison where she can get appropriate discipline. Once we prove this point to the hospital board, you will never have to worry about her hunting your family down again."

"So, when she goes to jail, she'll serve her full fifteen-year sentence?" Colby asked.

"Absolutely," I responded.

If not more, I thought, remembering Darla could be another one of Karma's casualties.

"I'll help you," Colby answered, finally giving me what I wanted to hear.

I spelled out the plan to him. The entire time his wife kept butting in, and I wanted to just send her ass home in a cab or something. When it was all said and done, Colby and I had worked out a deal in the name of keeping his family safe, and unbeknownst to him, saving my life.

Karma

26

---

*M*onday had been somewhat eventful, but nothing that I couldn't handle. At least now that Doc's secret was out, I could move on regarding WhiteKnight. And to think, I was starting to have feelings for the ol' guy. I guess Doc and WhiteKnight being one in the same explained how I could somewhat fall for the other man. Doc still had my heart though. He'd managed to make me forget all about Cole.

There used to be a time when I thought about Cole daily. At this point, he only crossed my mind periodically. Doc was the man in my life now. The difference between what I had with Cole and my relationship with Doc was that Doc and I were actually going to be married. The plans were in the making.

I was elated when the assistant, Julie, came to my room with security to let me know my lockdown had been lifted. *I knew my man wouldn't hold me down for long,* I thought. I smiled inside, realizing Doc wasn't as hard as he portrayed to be. If he didn't care about me or my feelings, he would've ordered an indefinite lockdown. Plus, he would've brought suspicion upon me regarding Darla's disappearance, but he hadn't.

Julie had been Darla's assistant ever since I'd come to True Hope. Whenever Darla was off or on work overload, Julie was the one to step in. It was a pleasure to once again see her little freckled face. I put on my shoes then was led to the library by Julie and a security officer.

There was one other person in the computer room— Mr. Brooks. He was as crazy as they come, but I think he'd heard from someone not to start stuff with me. He always cut up with the librarian, and as mean as she was, it was a wonder the poor man never got his library privileges revoked. He hardly ever spoke when he saw me. I waved at him then went to sit in front of my usual screen. He didn't wave back, but I didn't care.

I was so grateful to be out of my room and back in front of the computer, but I wasn't feeling like myself. I felt like my dinner had soured on my stomach. I sort of thought if I could regurgitate everything I ate the night before, I'd feel better. But there was no way I was going to ask to be excused. I wanted all the Internet time I could have.

I didn't know what I would do now that chatting with WhiteKnight wasn't an option. I decided to log into my email, which I hadn't done in a while either. Last time I was in that account, I sent an email to Doc that sent the lovely Ms. Aisha over the edge. *Perhaps I'll send Doc an email that would let Aisha have another eyeful.* When I laughed out loud, Mr. Brooks gave me the side-eye. I ignored him and continued logging into my account. Once it was opened, I weeded out the junk mail and ran across an email I just knew had to be a prank. The sender was Colby Patterson—the subject line read: WE NEED TO TALK.

I hurriedly opened the email to see if it was real.

Karma,

I know you haven't heard from me in a while, but I felt it was well-past time we reconnect. I was able to get your email from one of the nurses at the hospital when I called there over a month ago. I think she said her name was Darla. She said you couldn't receive visitors, but she gave me your email. I really wish we could talk face-to-face. There are so many things that need to be said and so much you need to know. If only you could somehow have passes from the facility, you could meet with me, so we could talk. It's too bad though, because I would've invited you to meet me this afternoon at the Beale Street Landing. I'm taking my family there at 3:00, and I've gotten permission from Nick's parents to bring Colbia along. Audrie won't be with us. She has other things on her schedule, but the kids and I will still have a great time.

Anyway, I'm hoping you'll see this email and return my message. Perhaps we can talk via phone sometimes. Just let me know. I'll look for your reply.

Take care,

Cole

Wow, was all I could think. Cole actually reached out to me. I wasn't prepared for this. After many nights, long ago, of wishing he would pay me some attention, there he was contacting me. It seemed Darla had some purpose after all. I really didn't know how to feel. Doc had my heart, but after reading Cole's email, some old feelings resurfaced. I began to wonder if he was as fine and sexy as I remembered. I needed to find a way to go and see him. Plus, Colbia would be there. Just thinking about being with the two of them again was exciting.

I must've read that email twenty times or more. Then, during one of the final reads, I had a notion that perhaps Doc was playing me again. *What if he's playing with my emotions again? Would Cole really reach out to me after all I've done? I had his first wife killed, and even killed his best friend myself. What could he possibly want to speak to me about?*

I read the email ten times more and realized the message had to be from Cole. He even mentioned what he would be doing later, and that the kids would be with him. I had to figure a way out of there to see for myself.

I waited until the library Grinch wasn't looking, and then I sneaked out. I headed down the hall to the laundry room, looking for something—anything that would disguise me. I spotted a stack of brand new, light-blue hospital scrubs and matching scrub hats. I fanned through the stack until I found my size, and sneaked off to my room to change and retrieve the keys to my Audi.

Once I changed, I peeped out of my room, down the hall to make sure everything was clear. It was, so I hurriedly walked down the hall to the side door. Once I got there, a security officer was pacing nearby. I could only hope he didn't recognize my face. Much of the rest of my body was covered by the scrubs and hat. I kept my head down as I approached the officer. To my surprise, he said good morning then stepped over to hold the door open for me. Rather than speak back, I nodded at the man then moved quickly out the door.

That was way too easy! I thought. I hurried around the front of the building then down the street to the nearby parking garage. As I approached the Audi, it seemed untouched. How the hell Memphis Police had been missing Darla's car was beyond me. Though in a garage, it was still in plain sight—near her job. I popped the trunk to make sure the items I'd stolen from Aisha were still there. I smiled as I admired my treasures then quickly reclosed the trunk so I could get out of there.

It was only 11:50 A.M., so I had plenty of time before Cole and the kids would be downtown. I headed there anyway. As I drove toward Memphis, my mouth kept watering—so much so that I kept rolling down the window to spit. I couldn't understand why. I wasn't hungry. In fact, I was feeling like Doc said he felt, and I didn't want anything to eat. My last psychiatrist told me that some-times your nerves would cause your body to react in strange ways. All I could think of was that perhaps I was overly excited about being able to see Cole and our family.

I parked the car once I arrived then got out to take a walk. I didn't want Cole to see me in scrubs, but it was either that or the formal, knee-length dress I wore to the gala. I surely couldn't let him see me in the other item I stole from Aisha's closet. Not only would he be puzzled, but he'd have questions that I wasn't prepared to answer. I just decided to stay in the scrubs.

After walking around, enjoying the fresh air and people-watching, I decided to take a seat on a bench. I'd only been there for close to an hour when I noticed Cole walking toward the Landing. I immediately jumped up, ready to run to him, but I decided to take it slow. I didn't want to scare the man. I paced myself, careful not to rush.

As I walked toward him, I noticed something wasn't right. He was a few hours early, and the children weren't with him. Why hadn't he brought the kids? He told me he'd have Colbia, but she was no where in site. This was a bit of a shock, so I slowed my pace even more. I had almost come to a complete stop, and it seemed as if I was moving in slow motion.

When Cole turned and looked toward the restaurant and nodded, my eyes followed the direction in which he looked. My soul nearly drained from my body as I was crushed to see Doc standing in the entryway. They met off to the side, seemingly discussing something important as they talked with their hands, pointing and using body language. This was clearly a setup, and somebody would have to pay for this.

I waited until the men finished talking and went their separate ways. They had to have been plotting how they would catch me down there, so Doc could have me sent to jail for leaving the premises of True Hope. I was very disappointed in Cole for trying to sabotage me, and it was time to let him know it.

As we walked straight toward each other, he didn't recognize me in the scrubs. He tried to go around me.

"Excuse me, ma'am," Cole said.

I walked right into his chest, knocking him backward a little, then said, "You're excused, muthafucker!"

His eyes widened, but for some reason he still didn't see my open palm getting ready to slam across his face. He didn't scream as I had expected, but he did wobble to the side in a daze. I had mustered up so much strength with that blow, it left me winded. The smack made such a loud noise that people nearby came to a complete halt, obviously in as much shock as Cole was. I looked up just in time to see Doc running to Cole's rescue.

I took off running before Doc could reach me. I glanced over my shoulder long enough to see him stop to make sure Cole was alright, and then he decided to chase after me. I didn't have far to go though. I was able to hop in my car and speed away from there before he could catch up to me and see what I was driving.

Well, I knew that was probably the last time I'd see Cole for a while, but I would deal with Doc once he got back to True Hope. He needed to learn a lesson once and for all about playing games with me. Oh, there would be hell to pay.

Lawrence

27

---

*T*he last thing I expected was for Karma to outsmart me on my plan. Cole and I had created a fictitious email account with his name on it and put the settings to let us know when Karma actually opened the message. When she didn't reply, we really didn't know whether she had fallen for the trick. I wish I could've had security with their eyes on her the entire morning, but that would defeat our plan to let her sneak out.

Had our whole plan worked, she would have talked with Cole for a bit, long enough for her to get comfortable, and then I would have notified the police and had them move in on her—the mental hospital escapee. Her escape would've been enough proof and reason to have her transferred elsewhere, but she had outsmarted me once again.

When I arrived back to True Hope, Karma was back in her room, pretending to be napping. I was livid by the time I made it there and asked the nursing staff to check on her. They reported back that she had complained of not feeling well and needed to rest. She was clever all right, but there had to be a way to beat her at her games. I needed to figure it out.

Steve came into my office around 3:00 P.M., wondering what I'd been up to all day. I told him the whole scheme from beginning to end. He couldn't believe his ears as he sat in front of me while I sat at my desk.

"So, when it's all said and done, she won again!" Steve said, shaking his head.

"Man, I had thought Darla must've been helping her, but hell, where is she?" I shrugged.

"Well, Darla isn't here, so it's evident nobody is helping her."

"Naw, man. Think about it. How'd she get out of here? Or, better yet, how'd she get back in without incident?"

Steve shrugged. "Good question, but she's always been slick, Lawrence. She stays on top of her game. All of this shit just seem so unreal to me—like something that only happens in the movies."

"Right! And you have no idea how tired I am. I'm mentally drained. I've been slacking on my other patients, and you already know about the destruction in my marriage. I can hardly get Aisha to say three words to me. She keeps saying she's looking for somewhere to live."

"I wondered about that—whether she had plans to leave."

"She doesn't trust me anymore, and I don't blame her, but more so than that, she's scared. Scared of what else

I'll do, and scared of what Karma will do. She has read about how Karma had Cole's first wife killed, you know."

"Yeah, I know, but didn't you know how dangerous this girl was before you started messing around with her?"

"Look. Let's not go there today. Yes, I knew, but I can't even begin to explain what was going on in my head, and I'm already drained for today. Let's just try to figure out something else, please."

A knock came on the door, and then it opened. Julie, Darla's assistant, peeped in.

"Dr. Weisman, I'm sorry to interrupt, but do you have a minute?" she asked.

"Yes, come in, Julie," I said.

"Good afternoon, Dr. Johnson," she said, nodding at Steve. "You don't have to leave. I just want to let Dr. Weisman know that Karma was taken to the nurse practitioner's office to be examined. She was complaining that she thought she might have Ebola."

"Ebola?" Steve and I both yelled.

Julie smiled. "Yes, I know it sounds ridiculous, but we told her we would have her examined since she insisted that she felt bad, and she has even been dry heaving."

"Julie," I said, "we all know full well there is nothing wrong with Karma besides wanting attention."

"Yes, I know, Dr. Weisman. Oh, and by the way, when the nurse practitioner asked how she thought she might've contracted Ebola, she said because Nurse Mitchell had recently been out of the country. She even went as far as saying Nurse Mitchell was probably somewhere quarantined due to having Ebola."

"Ridiculous," I responded, "but thanks for letting me know all of this. I'm going to put it in my notes. Be sure to keep me posted on her results from the nurse."

"Okay. I sure will," Julie said as she turned to leave.

Steve and I just stared at each other until the door closed. I shook my head and let out an exasperated breath.

"So, what do you think she's up to now?" Steve asked.

"That was the question I was just about to ask you. Can you please help me figure this bitch out?"

"Lawrence, man, I don't know how in the hell you were stupid enough to go between that girl's legs. She is a master manipulator!"

"Look. How is Barbara? Do you think she will keep all of this on the low?"

"Yeah. She won't spill the beans—not because she's looking out for you, but because of me and because Aisha's her friend."

"Okay. Cool. Well, I had to have another conversation with Mr. Patterson once I made it back to the office."

"Yeah? Well, how did that go?"

"He's upset, and rightfully so. I mean, his wife didn't want him to have anything to do with the ploy in the first place. Now he has to find a way to tell her our plan didn't work, and I can only imagine how unsafe she's going to feel."

"Call him back and tell him the paperwork is being processed now."

"Man, I don't wanna lie. What happens when he realizes I hadn't gotten anything done?"

"Then you tell him there has been some delays, but you keep assuring him things are working out."

I shook my head. "I hear you. I guess that's my only option. And to think, I almost told him everything."

"Wow . . . aren't you glad you didn't?"

"Yeah, I owe his wife a big thank-you for showing up to dinner because had I told him the whole story between Karma and me, that might've put the final nail in my coffin."

"I'm so glad you know, my friend."

There was another knock at the door, and Julie just walked right in afterwards. "Dr. Weisman, I have some bad news and more bad news."

I stood and walked around my desk to meet her face-to-face. "Okay, Julie, what is it?"

"Sir, it's been reported on the news that Nurse Mitchell's body has been found. Someone dumped her in the river."

My heart sank. Steve eased out of the chair and stared at Julie blankly. I, too, was at a loss for words. Julie's eyes began to water, and she stood in front of us, blinking back tears. I had a lump in my throat, but I managed to speak again.

"Julie, you said you had more bad news. Is there more to this?"

"Um, not to this, Dr. Weisman," she said, "but there is more bad news regarding a patient. We'll need to speak in private for this one."

I turned to Steve and raised an eyebrow. I meant to give him an oh-no-not-Ms.-Trouble-again look, but he must've perceived me to be asking for pardon. He patted me on the shoulder then started out the door.

"We'll talk more on those documents later, Dr. Weisman," he said.

"Sure thing, Dr. Johnson."

Julie waited for Steve to walk out and close the door before she spoke again. She patted underneath her eye to dry the hint of tears that created a damp lining, and then I demanded she hit me with it.

"What is it, Julie?"

"Dr. Weisman, the nurse practitioner examined Karma for a number of things—just to make sure she was all right."

"Ok. What's wrong?"

"Well, all of her vitals were good, and her cultures for Strep throat came back fine."

"Well, what didn't?"

"Dr. Weisman, Karma is pregnant."

Say something, I told myself. *Anything, Fool! You're going to give yourself away, if you don't say something.* In my mind, I had broken down on my knees in tears, right in front of Julie. That's exactly what I felt like. I had spoken with Steve earlier about the last nail in my coffin—but now I realize telling Cole my business wouldn't have been it. Learning Karma was pregnant was, and my once-perfect life was as good as dead.

Karma

28

A knock came on my door, and then it opened. It was pretty late in the evening, and I had already told Julie I wasn't going outside. I wasn't feeling well, and now I knew why. *Pregnant? Why didn't I guess that before?* It wasn't like Doc and I was using protection, but I'd been told I wouldn't be able to have any more kids due to a feminine procedure I'd had.

Only one month after being in True Hope, I experienced severe cramps and heavy bleeding. I was taken to the doctor, and after an examination and an MRI, it was determined I had uterine fibroids. Three weeks later, I found myself on an operating table, having an UFE — the Uterine Fibroid Embolization. I was told that having this procedure would block the blood flow to the fibroids, which would cause them to shrink, but that the aftermath would be premature menopause. I was so sure the UFE had thrown me into the "change" as my late maternal grandmother used to call it, simply because I didn't get another menstrual cycle after the procedure.

Although she knew I wasn't feeling well, Julie came walking into my room, demanding I get up and put some clothes on. I continued to lay there as if she hadn't said a word. The nerve of her!

"Why?" I asked. "Didn't I already tell you I don't wanna go outside today? And I told Tee I'd catch up with her tomorrow."

"We're not going outside. Some very important people need to see you."

"Like who?"

"Just get up," she said, tugging on my arm as I refused to budge. "C'mon, Karma, let's not go through this today."

"Okay, okay," I said. "Let my arm go, Ms. Julie. You're stressing the baby."

Julie shook her head at me. "How'd you get pregnant anyway? Ain't many men around here except the male patients who are old enough to be your grand-daddy—and I know you're not fooling with either of them."

"How could you be so sure? Isn't their money green?" I gave her a blank stare.

Julie frowned so hard, she looked as if she was about to regurgitate. I eased a smile on my face despite how sickly I felt then got up to dress. That's what the bitch get for questioning me. I mean, I like 'em mature, but hell, not ancient. No retired grandpas for me.

After getting some clothes on, Julie and Herman, one of the security officers I hadn't seen in a while, walked me down the hall toward the small conference room. On the way there, I was doing celebratory back flips in my mind.

Pregnant? was all I kept thinking. *Pregnant? And by the good doctor? Wow!* This news was huge! It was definitely time to put my plan into play, so Doc and I could get married. I couldn't believe my luck—I actually had another chance to be married and have a family. Soon, I would be the one true Mrs. Lawrence Weisman.

Julie opened the conference room door and led me in to meet two suited people with badges. I looked back at Julie, waiting for her to explain.

"Karma, these people are detectives, and they'd like to ask you a few questions, if you don't mind," she said.

"Of course. Why would I mind?" I asked. "But may I ask what this is about?"

The tall dark one with the smooth, deep voice like the man on the Allstate commercials spoke up. "Ms. Jolley, we're homicide detectives—I'm McKnight and this is my partner," he said, nodding toward the woman with the pretty fingernails and flawless makeup. I'd seen her before, but I couldn't put my finger on it. He continued. "We're investigating the murder of Ms. Darla Mitchell."

"And . . . so, why do you want to talk to me?" I asked.

The woman stood firm with her hands in her pockets. "Well, we're going to have a chat with as many people around here as we can, Ms Jolley, but as for now, we need you to cooperate, so we can get you out of here and move on to the next interview. Fair enough?"

As I stared into her eyes, I suddenly realized who this woman was. She was the homicide detective I'd seen on that cop show in the Memphis episodes! This female was a no-nonsense, tough-talking, I'ma-get-to-the-bottom-of-this-shit kinda woman. I knew I needed to come correct with her if I wanted to get back out of that room without handcuffs. I answered her politely.

"Sure. Yes, ma'am. Fair enough," I said then took a seat at the table.

"So, Ms. Jolley," Detective McKnight started, "What type of relationship did you have with Ms. Mitchell?"

"Relationship?" I asked. "I wouldn't call it a relationship, unless you're counting the fact that she was the main nurse who took care of me on the dayshift."

"So, there was no friendship of some sort beyond what you're saying?" his partner asked.

"No, why would she and I need to be friends?" I stared at her unblinkingly.

"You let us ask all the questions, Ms. Jolley," she said. "You just cooperate and give us answers, or else we're gonna be here all night. And I ain't got nothing but time." She looked at the watch on her arm and nodded.

"Well, I don't have all the time you have, so come on with the next question," I responded.

Detective McKnight's smooth voice interjected. "You don't have time? What do you have to do that's so important?"

"My bed is calling me," I said simply.

"Oh, I see," Detective McKnight said. "We're inter-rupting your nap time. Well, let's hurry right along. This little girl needs her nap," he said while smirking at his partner.

"I'm pregnant, you asshole!" I blurted. "And I happen to not be feeling well."

They gave me an incredulous look, seemingly taken aback by my revelation. Detective McKnight opened and closed his mouth a few times in an apparent attempt to say something, but he couldn't seem to form the right words. After several awkward moments of silence, he finally said something, but it wasn't to me.

"Is she for real?" he asked Julie.

Julie's face was red. She never parted her lips, only nodded. Hell, I couldn't understand what her embarrass-ment was about. It wasn't as if she was the one who got me pregnant. But of course, I could understand that maybe she figured the detectives would be looking upon her funny because somehow I'd managed to get pregnant under all of the staff's care. McKnight's partner spoke up.

"Well, listen," she said. "We're not going to hold you long. Just a few more questions."

Just then, the door opened and I was so elated to see it was my man. He paused at the door, not saying a word. For a caramel-complexioned man, his face looked as if all of his blood had drained. I'd never seen him so white before. He glanced around the room and even made eye contact with me. The panic on his face was so evident, Julie had to address him.

"Dr. Weisman, are you all right?" Julie asked.

He seemed to have snapped out of whatever had him gripped in fear. "Um, yeah, yeah," he said, fully entering the room and closing the door behind him. "I'm fine. So, what's going on here?"

I elected to be the one to explain. "Well, this is Detective McKnight and his partner here, and they're conducting a murder investigation—can you believe that?"

Doc walked over and shook the detectives' hands. He introduced himself, stating he was my psychiatrist and that someone from the hospital had called him from home, requesting his presence. I guess whoever called him did the right thing because everyone at True Hope knew I would act a fool whenever I was ready. McKnight started more questioning.

"Dr. Weisman, are you aware that Karma is pregnant?" McKnight asked.

Doc cleared his throat. I could've sworn tiny beads suddenly appeared on his bald head. He repeatedly brushed his hand down his salt-and-pepper goatee as he answered.

"Um, yes. I was made aware of that earlier today," he answered.

I smiled as I swiveled side to side in my chair. I loved this line of questioning. The detective continued.

"Well, I'm sure you will get to the bottom of that, but as for now, we're here to investigate what might have happened to Darla Mitchell," McKnight said. "Dr. Weisman, are you aware Ms. Jolley has been seen on the security videos, having private conversations with Ms. Mitchell?"

He looked stumped, and truth be told, so was I. I had forgotten all about someone could have the video tapes pulled.

"No. I wasn't aware of that," Doc answered.

"Are you aware of any special friendship or relationship Ms. Jolley might've had with Ms. Mitchell," Long Fingernails asked.

Doc glanced at me briefly. "No, not at all."

"Ms. Jolley, what were you and Ms. Mitchell talking about on the videos?" McKnight asked.

"I don't know," I answered.

"What do you mean, you don't know?" McKnight pressed. "Again, Ms. Jolley, we can be here all night, if that's the game you want to play."

"Look," I blurted. "Ms. Mitchell and I have had many conversations. I don't which conversations you're referring to."

McKnight began ruffling papers, and then stopped when he found one he might've been looking for. "How about the conversation you were seen having with her last week?"

"Oh, that was last week. I don't remember." I smiled.

Both detectives sighed heavily. I wanted to laugh in their faces, but when I looked over at Doc, he seemed nervous. He slightly shook his head, begging on a sly for me to behave. I placed my hand over my mouth, hoping he'd understand that I wouldn't say anything out of line—well, that was only if he behaved, too.

Low and behold, my man disappointed me. He decided to play detective himself, or was it that he had become just that curious about what Darla and I talked about? Either way, he should've waited and asked me later because the minute he decided to play a game of Who Can Embarrass Who, I won.

"So, Karma, why did Ms. Mitchell take you off to the side for discussion?" Doc asked.

"I don't know," I responded. "That's a question you'd have to ask her—oops, but I forgot—she's dead."

"Karma, that's nothing to joke about," Doc said.

"Who's joking? She is dead, isn't she?" I glanced around the room as if I wanted someone to agree.

"Listen, Karma," Doc said. "The detectives are asking about that conversation because it could be critical to finding out who killed Ms. Mitchell. Did she say anything about where she was going or who she would be with?"

That was it! He should've quit while he was ahead. It was clear I didn't want to talk to the detectives about that conversation, but now it was time for me to show out.

"Okay . . . since you all must know . . . here it is!" I sat straight up in my chair. "Ms. Mitchell confided in me that she'd had a baby in confidence—by someone here on staff—"

"Wait, wait, wait," Doc interrupted. "Maybe that is a little too personal, Karma. I think the detectives only want to know the part of the conversation that might deal with what her plans were for the night."

"Naw, Dr. Weisman," I responded, staring unblinkingly into Doc's eyes. "I believe the detectives would like to hear the whole story—from beginning to end!"

"Hold on," Long Fingernails said. "We do want to hear the whole story, but there is no need to yell and be hostile, Ms. Jolley."

I clutched my side and jumped out of my seat. "Oooooww!" I screamed.

Julie came to my side. "What's wrong, Karma?"

"My side . . . it hurts. Oooooowww!" I yelled again.

"Do you think you need to go to the emergency room?" Julie asked.

I nodded and panted rather than spoke. And just like that, the interrogation was over. I'm sure the detectives figured they could just come to the hospital to finish their line of questioning, or perhaps just revisit True Hope another day, but I had plans of my own. I had somewhere to be by the next day, so it was time to set things in motion.

The EMT's rolled me into the Baptist Memorial Hospital's emergency room on Capital Way—not where I wanted to go. I tried so hard to convince them I needed to be at a hospital in Memphis, but they wouldn't hear of it. They claimed Baptist Memorial was Doc's request, plus the fault of my insurance. My insurance should've covered at 100% wherever I chose to go, but since I hadn't done my homework on that, I couldn't argue with anyone.

I wasn't in any pain. I don't know why so many people kept falling for my shit, but for the sake of my plans, it was good that they did. As I lay on the hospital bed with IVs connected to my veins, I laughed to myself about how full of it the doctors were. They couldn't find anything wrong with me, but for the sake of making money, they claimed I was a little dehydrated and hooked me up to some fluids. Dehydrated or not—I hadn't planned on staying at that hospital.

When the last nurse left my room, I unhooked myself, slid my skinny jeans and top back on, and found my pair of New Balance gym shoes under the bed. Julie was so dumb to get them for me when I asked just before being lifted into the ambulance. My excuse was that I didn't want to wear my slippers to the ER. Had Doc been close by, he might've figured out my scheme the moment I asked for my tennis shoes.

I tied double knots in my shoes, making sure they'd stay tied once I got on the run. I peeped into the hallway and saw that the nurse station was busy with people, and the guard's back was turned as he spoke on a cell phone. I hurriedly went down the hall the opposite way. I was actually headed in the right direction because once I turned the corner, I saw the entryway to the ER.

On my way out of the ER, I spotted Doc on his way in. His eyes were buried into his cell phone, so this afforded me the opportunity to take a seat. I grabbed a magazine someone had left in a nearby chair and hid my face as Doc questioned the woman at the check-in desk. It appeared she gave him directions, and then he walked off into the hallway I'd just escaped.

I watched the back him as he walked off. I was happily on my way out of Baptist Memorial and back to where I'd stashed Darla's—I mean, my car.

Lawrence

29

*T*hat damn Karma—what could I say about her? She'd shown me how clever she was since day one. How she managed to escape the hospital, getting right by me, I just don't know. I was in my office the next morning, trying to figure out my next move. Last I'd heard, the police still hadn't located her, so not only was Cole and his family in danger, but so was my household.

Aisha was devastated to know Karma was on the loose again. She insisted she would not stay at the house with me unless Karma was captured. I gave her my American Express Gold Card and told her to go ahead and book a room at the Westin Memphis Beale Street hotel. She graciously accepted my card, but told me I could not stay with her. I slept at the house all night, practically with one eye open.

I needed some coffee, tea, or whatever would help me stay alert in my office. Not having slept well was taking a toll on me. My eyes seemed to be crossing together as I checked email after email. As I scrolled through my account, a new message popped up from Aisha. I opened it immediately.

Hi babe,

I know you weren't expecting an email from me this morning, but I felt we needed to talk. It's been rough between us ever since I found out about you and that Karma girl, and I was thinking perhaps we need some time to ourselves to clear the air. I'm not ready for things to be over between us, and I know you aren't either. So, what do you say we have a little rendezvous up in the mountains for a few days? I will book our favorite cabin. All you need to do is take the time off work, starting tonight, and meet me up there. I really want to focus on getting back to us — you know, when we were happy. I love you, babe.

See you soon!

Aisha

Wow! This is a change, I thought. I picked up the phone to call Aisha, but then put it back down. I read her email again and thought that perhaps she just wanted me to respond in email, and then just show up. I wrote her back.

Hey sweetie,

Yes, your message was a pleasant surprise. I will be more than willing to take off work and meet you at our spot. I think you're right. We do need some time alone to sort things out. Aisha, I know I hurt you, but baby, I promise we can get through this. I also promise to never hurt you again. I was so wrong, and if I could take it all back I would. I love you, too, baby, and I'm looking forward to getting up in those mountains with you.

See you soon . . . love you!

Larry

After sending my response, I couldn't stop thinking about Aisha. We used to be so in love, and I was ready to get back to the "us" she was talking about in her email. I went back to her message and read it a third time. This time, I realized she hadn't put a time to meet her, so I picked up the phone to call her.

"Hello," she answered softly.

"Hi, sweetie, were you asleep?"

"No, I was just about to call you."

I smiled inside. "You were? Are you okay?"

"Mm-hmm. I'm fine. I was just reading your email."

"Oh, you got it already?"

"Yeah. I got it."

"So, what are you thinking?"

"I don't know," she said somberly. "I'm just ready to get away from here. Really anywhere would be nice—as long as it's far away from that girl."

"I know, sweetheart, and let's not talk of her. We need to focus on us. Okay?"

She paused, but then said, "I hear you."

"So what time should we leave?"

"I'm checking out of this hotel in a minute. I plan to go shopping for an hour or so, and then I'm hitting the road."

"You sure you don't want to wait and ride with me?"

"No, I'll be fine. The drive alone will do me some good. I really just need to clear my head."

"Okay, sweetie. Go ahead and use that gold card to check in once you get there. I'll be leaving here early myself. I need to get home and pack a bag. I'll see you later on."

"I'll call you to let you know when I've made it."

"Great. Thanks, baby."

"Okay. Bye," she said then hung up.

I had hoped to get an "I love you" before getting off the phone, but that was out. Though I was disappointed, I figured at least Aisha and I were on the same page again and would be adding new chapters to our story—or so I thought. What I hadn't counted on was more drama and another rude awakening, but that's exactly what I got. In fact, I needed to snatch my own medical license away and all of my degrees, too, because an educated man wouldn't have ever fallen for the things I did. And only a dumb ass would have fallen for what awaited me next.

Karma

30

As I combed the entire cabin, I could see why Doc and Aisha loved making the four-hundred-and-nine mile trip up to Pigeon Forge, Tennessee. Their favorite cabin was amazing. It was totally worth it to order that software many months ago. It helped me tap into people's email. I was able to see some of Doc's credit card information as well as trips he'd booked in the past. I found confirmations to two different secluded spots he liked to frequent, and I could only assume he visited them with his wife.

Once I got my plan together, I decided to schedule emails—one going from Doc to Aisha, and the other going from Aisha to Doc. Doc's email to Aisha stated that he wanted to meet her at their favorite secluded spot in Compton, Arkansas. Aisha's email to him stated they should meet at their cabin in Pigeon Forge, Tennessee. Boy, they were in for a surprise.

I was totally tickled at the fact that I'd sent Aisha six hours away from their home in Collierville, which meant even if she wanted to find Doc, she would have nearly eleven hours before she could reach us—and that's after she would have driven the six hours into Arkansas. How clever am I? Very, I'd say!

The mountains were breathtakingly beautiful. The ranger that helped me get to the cabin called me Mrs. Weisman after I signed Doc's check-in statement and retrieved the keys to the cabin. He stressed that Doc himself needed to make the check-out. I smiled politely and assured the man that he would. I tipped the ranger with the money I'd found stashed in Darla's purse she'd left in the car and asked if he'd arrange for a minister or justice of the peace to come to the cabin in a few hours. When he mentioned he knew someone who could renew our vows, I remembered I was supposed to be Aisha and was married already. I smiled then closed the door.

After roaming the cabin, I discovered there were two master suites, three full baths, a game room, an indoor Jacuzzi, satellite TVs, a spacious kitchen, a living room and fully equipped bar area, and multiple fireplaces that I wasn't so sure we would use unless the temperature dropped drastically at night. Although the entire cabin was one level, one of the master suites sat just off the hill, so there was a large patio extended outside of it. I stepped out there and the view nearly took my breath away. There was an all-white gazebo, strategically placed amongst the array of trees and their many variations of green. There also was a small stream, which quietly flow less than one hundred feet away from the cabin. This made things so surreal for me. In only a few hours, I would have said my vows and become Mrs. Lawrence Weisman.

I turned to go back inside and began unpacking all of the items I'd stolen from Aisha's closet and bathroom. I safely hid my black Audi, so once Doc arrived, he wouldn't be suspicious. I set out the items I'd purchased just before making it to Pigeon Forge. I bought candles, flowers, chocolates, strawberries, champagne flutes and champagne, and a small wedding cake. If I could thank Darla for keeping so much cash in her purse, I would. Maybe she was about to pay a bill. It didn't matter. I was just happy that the money served me well.

After lighting the candles and placing rose petals all over the living room, I set two filled champagne flutes on the coffee table. Next to them, I placed some strawberries, chocolates, and a snack mix. I knew he might be hungry once he got in, but we had the business of our wedding to attend to before we went out to eat. The snack mix would pacify him, and then he'd want to take a sip of my special champagne. The thought of it made me smile. I wondered how he'd feel once he saw my wedding dress.

It was time for me to get ready. I went inside the master suite I'd chosen—the one with the patio—then stepped into the bathroom to get ready.

I had just stepped out of the shower when I heard him calling to me through the bathroom door.

"Hey, babe," he said. "You okay?"

"Mm-hmm," I answered.

"All right. I just wanted you to know I made it. Thanks for leaving the door unlocked."

"Mm-hmm," I responded.

"What're you doing? Brushing your teeth?"

"Mm-hmm."

"Okay. Hey, I'm going to go ahead and have some champagne since you've poured it."

"Mm-hmm."

"Oh, and why do you have your wedding dress stretched across the bed like that?"

"Mmm," was all I said.

"Never mind. I forgot you were brushing your teeth. You can explain it to me later. Oh, I didn't see your car out there. I guess you sent it to be service, right?"

"Mm-hmm."

"Okay. See you when you come out."

"Mm-hmm."

Boy was he dumb. He walked away and didn't bother to ask me to open the door. Geez. He sure made my scheme easy.

I waited until I figured he'd had at least one glass of my special champagne, which was laced with a mixture of sleeping pills and Cialis, the drug used to treat erectile dysfunctions. I had sneaked it out of the nurse practitioner's medical cabinet when I visited her office. I had heard that some of the temporary patients were allowed to use it when necessary during conjugal visits. I was too happy to open that cabinet and see a stash of the pills there.

After drying myself off and putting on Aisha's smell goods, I wrapped myself back up in the plush, white towel provided by the cabin, and then tiptoed toward the living room. I stood quietly off to the side and watched Doc, sitting on the sofa in front of the TV with his half-empty champagne flute up to his mouth. He frowned a little once he gulped the last swallow then held the glass up to look at it. I wondered if he had spotted some residue from the pills, but when he set the glass down on the coffee table and refilled his glass, I knew I was off the hook.

The second glass did it. Doc began nodding off on the sofa. His head jerked many times as he nodded, waking him up each time. He leaned back and closed his eyes. I watched as he slid his hand to his midsection to situate his erection. After several unsuccessful attempts to relocate the massive bulge, I watched him unzip his pants and massage himself, causing a greater swelling under-neath his briefs. I knew he needed relief, and it was well-past time I help him.

I walked over to the sofa then dropped my towel. Doc could hardly open his eyes.

"Aisha, baby, you're wearing my favorite perfume," he said, squinting. "So, you found it after all."

I didn't respond to him. Instead, I kneeled and began pulling off his pants. He was still wearing his shoes, so I was only able to pull his pants to his ankles. He was groggy, but was fully aware what was going on.

"Sweetie, we should go to the bedroom," he said. "Let's go to—"

That was all he could say before I eased him into my mouth. He surprised me with deep, roaring moans. I was only used to the muffled sounds he'd make in his office, trying not to get caught. But we were free in this place—

free to be as loud as we wanted to be. I took more of him into my throat, hoping for more sounds of pleasure, and that's just what he gave me. I wasn't worried about him exploding. I knew those erectile dysfunction pills would have him going for hours. He panted as he spoke.

"Aisha," he said. "Aisha, baby. Hold on, baby. That feels so good, but—"

"But what, baby?" I asked, taking him by surprise as I hopped on top of him.

He caught on to my voice and tried to collect himself, but it was of no use. My special champagne rendered him into my mercy. But I had no mercy for him. I needed him, and his thick, ten-inch rod needed me. As I straddled him with him deep inside me, I stuck my tongue into his mouth and did a slow-wind. He struggled a little at first, but he was too weak to fight. Besides, juicy had him crazy. I took my tongue out of his mouth then squeezed my muscles tight around his dick.

"Karma," he panted. "What the fuck are you doing here?"

"I told you we'd be together, and this time it's forever, baby."

"Where's my wife?"

"That bitch is old news."

He panted and tried to struggle some more, but I held on firm to him, pending his hands down to his sides.

"You killed my wife?"

"Not yet."

"Not yet? What did you do with my wife? Where is she?" Doc said through tears.

I looked at the streaming tears on his face and became angry. "Un-un, mutherfucker, don't you start that shit. I didn't fall in love with no punk. You will *not* cry in my presence!"

"Just tell me if my wife is dead, bitch!"

"No! She's not dead, but you and Aisha are done! You hear me? You and I are going to be married in an hour or so, and we're going to live happily ever after!"

"Karma, what do you think you're doing with me?"

"You can't tell? I'm taking you into ecstasy," I responded as I began a faster grind, rolling my hips in circular motions.

Taking him in this way felt good, but I wanted more control and better leverage, so I forced him down onto the sofa. He was just like a pushover—no fight in him at all—just his words.

"Karma, stop it, damn. Get the fuck off me!"

"No, baby. You don't want that. You want more of this."

As I held him down, I began thrusting up and down on him. Two minutes later, he was moaning in pleasure. Ten minutes later, he was begging me to stop again. I couldn't stop. My juices were pouring, and I couldn't seem to get enough of him. He'd had one orgasm, and I'd had two when he finally said something that made me stop.

"Karma," he panted underneath me. I didn't answer. "Karma."

"What!"

"Think about what you're doing to our baby, sweetheart."

"What?"

"What're you doing to our unborn child with all of this rough sex?"

I hadn't thought about that. I stopped momentarily and wondered if I'd done any harm to our baby with too much motion. I began another slow grind, but Doc asked me to stop again.

"Karma, baby, this can't go on. Let's take a break. I thought you said a minister would be here to marry us soon."

"Yeah."

"Then, let's break, sweetheart. You need to get dressed."

That made me smile. I got up then pulled him up, but he plopped back down like a dead fish. When I attempted to pull him up again, he plopped back onto the sofa once again. This time, I heard him snoring.

I left him on the sofa and went to take another shower. I had to make sure I was nothing less than beautiful on my wedding day. It was so kind of Doc to remind me we had a visitor coming to administer our vows.

As I fixed my hair, using Aisha's expensive CHI flat iron, I peeped in on Doc from time to time. He was completely out of it. I made up my face, and then put on Aisha's long-ass wedding gown. She was slim, but she was tall as hell, and that dress, although very elegant, was too damn long. I kept tripping over my own feet. I stood in the long mirror in the bathroom and took a look at myself. I looked like a little girl playing dress up.

ALISHA YVONNE

"Fuck it," I said aloud. "This will have to do."

I didn't have heels I could wear, so I just headed to the living room barefooted. I could hardly walk. Between the tightness and the length of the dress, it was too much.

By the time I made it to the sofa to wake Doc, the doorbell rang. I looked over at my man. His pants were still at his ankles, so I inched over to him.

"Just a minute," I yelled to the visitor.

Before I could pull up Doc's pants, the front door collapsed in a thunderous crash. I was startled and tripped over my dress. The shouting voices alarmed me more.

"Freeze! Police!" the rough male voices said.

When I looked up and saw several armed officers entering the cabin, I knew I needed to get out of there by any means necessary. I scrambled to my feet then charged toward the door, but I ended up rolling like a human bowling ball, knocking over several policemen in my way. That didn't help me though. I was still apprehended before I could completely get out of the door.

While handcuffed and sitting in the back of a police car, another vehicle pulled up and out ran Aisha toward the cabin. How she got there so fast, I really didn't know. All I could think was perhaps she figured out my scheme long before she made it to Compton, Arkansas. Oh, well. The bitch still couldn't have my man. I was having his baby—not her.

I watched as Doc staggered toward Aisha with a policeman at his side. I listened intently through the cracked window as Aisha told them she figured something was wrong only thirty minutes into her drive when Doc

263

wouldn't answer his cell. She had OnStar locate his vehicle, and that's when she knew I must've been up to something. She shook her head as Doc explained how he believed I hacked their email accounts to get my way. She stopped listening when one of the officers asked a pertinent question.

"Is it true Ms. Jolley is pregnant? an officer asked. "She said she was pregnant as we placed her in the squad car."

"Um, well . . . um," Doc started.

"Um what?" Aisha asked. "Is she pregnant or not, Larry?"

"Um, yeah," he answered, avoiding eye contact with her.

She placed her hand on her hip. "Is it yours?"

The officer looked blown away by that question. His eyes moved back and forth between the two of them as if he was watching a close tennis match. Aisha demanded an answer.

"Well, is it?"

"Yeah," Doc answered softly.

"Hmph. First, I get a call on the way here from a Detective McKnight, asking if I knew about your child with that nurse that came up missing at True Hope, and now here you are admitting another possible baby?"

Doc remained silent and dropped his head. His eyes pleaded for forgiveness though.

Aisha shook her head at him then glanced over at me and said, "I'm sorry he did this to you."

I didn't respond. I didn't know how. I watched Aisha as she turned and walked toward the small steps that led to the cabin's entrance. Doc didn't see what I saw coming. Aisha picked up a ceramic frog about the size of a cantaloupe and smashed it on top of Doc's head before I could yell for him to watch out. Doc fell flat. The policeman grabbed Aisha, but she didn't resist. In fact, she only had a few words for the officer.

"You can arrest me now," she said. "But in our vows, we did say, 'Until death do us part.' And I hope the mutherfucker is dead."

Epilogue

(Three months later)

I'd been to The Criminal Justice Center a number of times, but I never expected one day it could be home for me. It was a damn shame I couldn't get Aisha or any of my family to post bond for me, and it was taking forever to even get a preliminary hearing. Sure, I was guilty, but I'd seen doctors and other people do far worse things than me and not have any incarceration. Why my bail was set at half a million dollars was beyond me. The only thing I could think of was that the judge wanted to make an example out of me. I just wanted to plead guilty, get a slap on the wrist and move on with my life. My medical license had been taken, so the worse had been done to me already.

Aisha was done with me, too—just like the medical industry. I thought we had made vows that said, "For better or worse and until death do us part," but she made it painfully obvious that she preferred the "until death do us part" clause. My beloved wife had produced a head wound on me that required fifteen medical stitches. I will never admit I deserved that, but I can admit I understood her anger. She'd wanted children for a while, and I can imagine she was reduced to feeling her lowest at the moment of hearing of my possible child with Darla and the one on the way with Karma.

It was visiting day, and although I placed several names on my list, the only person who had come to see me a few times was my attorney. So, imagine my disbelief when I was told there was a visitor who wanted to see me. I knew it couldn't be my attorney because he didn't come on visiting day, and he had just left the day before, declaring it would be at least another week before he'd be back.

I happily jumped off my cot, wearing my orange jumpsuit and followed the deputy to a room with multiple seats that were divided by short walls for privacy. He led me to a seat on the end of the room. I sat, staring at an empty chair on the other side of the glass window, wondering if the deputy had made a mistake. I turned to look at him.

"Just hold on," he said. "Your visitor is being escorted in now."

I nodded then waited, anxiously racking my mind over who the visitor could be. *Could it be Aisha?* Had my wife come to her senses and realized we still had so much living to do? Maybe not. I hadn't been able to get Aisha to answer my calls the whole three months I'd been locked down.

Then, I thought perhaps it could be my one and only brother who claimed he'd never visit me as long as I was housed at 201 Poplar. The Criminal Justice Center was a place he hated with a passion due to a fight he had one time while standing in line for traffic court. The man my brother fought had pushed him for demanding he not skip the line. The fight landed my brother in one of the cells I was now living in. I didn't know who the visitor was. I could only hope until the person got there.

The moment had finally arrived. Someone had walked to the end and pulled back the chair. After having taken a seat, I saw that it was Steve. I smiled then placed my fist against the window for him to reciprocate, but he didn't. My smile quickly went away as I felt he must have come with some sort of bad news. *How much more can I take?* I wondered. He picked up the phone on his side of the wall.

"What's wrong, man?" I asked after picking up my phone.

He shook his head. "Nothing. You a'ight?"

"Yeah. Just a little puzzled though. You got something to tell me? You upset about something?"

"Man, I'm good. I'm just trying to get used to the view in front of me. I mean, I knew someday it would come to this, considering the shit you'd done, but this is still very different for me."

I nodded. "I know what you mean. Imagine being me, if you want to know what difficult is."

"You talked to Aisha?"

"She won't answer my calls. Have you seen or talked to her?"

"Yeah. She's moving on, man."

"What do you mean, 'moving on?' Aisha and I haven't settled anything."

"Try telling that to her. She's still in the house, but from what I hear, she's prepared to move and sell at any minute."

"She can't do that without my signature!"

"Look don't shoot me. I'm just telling you what she told Barbara and me."

I sighed heavily. This was not what I wanted to hear from him. We were both quiet for a moment, and then I figured I better ask about my nemesis.

"So, any news about Karma?" I asked.

"From what I've read, she's been sent to Delta Charter Mental Health Center in Jackson, Mississippi. I believe it's temporary though. I don't know where she'll be shipped to next."

I shook my head. "I still don't know who could've been helping that girl. I wish I could chat with the members of surveillance. I need to get my hands on some video that would prove someone was working with her to set me up. If I can prove a setup, that might help me get a slap on the wrist."

Steve looked disgusted. "Lawrence, you're just as sick as Karma, I see. I don't even know why I bothered to come down here."

"Huh? What? What's wrong with checking with the surveillance team?"

"There's no need. I helped Karma."

I was sure I didn't hear him correctly. He couldn't have said what I thought I heard him say. My head shook rapidly as I disputed him.

"Naw. Un-un. You didn't just say that, I know," I said. "You wouldn't have set me up like that."

"Man, nobody set you up. You set your own ass up. You should've stopped fucking her when I told you to."

"Steve, what the fuck are you saying?"

"I'm saying, the only thing I did was try to make sure a woman with a real mental illness stayed ahead. She didn't deserve the crap you were doing to her. I called your house and your wife's cell phone to irritate the shit out of both of you because I needed you to wake up to the shit you were doing. I trashed your office—not Karma—because I wanted to scare your ass into quickly getting her out of your care. I looked out for her and let her back into the building some of the times she sneaked out of True Hope because she didn't deserve the trouble you were giving her. You were setting her up, and ready to hang her out to dry when you knew she was only acting out because of the mixed messages you were giving her. That girl needed real psychiatric help without a selfish-ass, horny-ass, so-called mutherfucking psychiatrist running up in her every time he laid eyes on her."

I was seething by now. "You muther—"

"No, Lawrence! You were one first. Somebody had to be on Karma's side, and I decided it had to be me."

He stood up to leave and started to put the phone back on the wall, but stopped.

"Oh, there are a couple of more things I think I should tell you: Your wife has a new man." My mouth nearly hit the floor. "Yeah. Shocking, I know. After learning about Darla's kid and Karma's pregnancy, Aisha said it was her turn to do something reckless. She's had this man at your house and in your bed."

"Steve, you can't let her do this, man."

"Who am I to stop her after all you've done?"

I dropped my head. My heart was heavy. When I looked up, Steve shot me another stinging blow.

"Oh, and the other thing you should know," he said, "I've been granted pardon to tell everything I know in court." As my mouth opened again, he finished. "That's right—I'm testifying against you."

He slammed the phone on the wall then walked away. I wasn't sure if he could hear me, but I called after him.

"Steve!" I yelled as I stood and watched him keep walking. "Steve, dammit, get your ass back here! Steve!"

The deputy who had led me to my seat insisted that I get back to my cell. I knew Steve wouldn't walk back there, but I just wasn't ready to give up. Once I saw that Steve was out the door on the other end, I relented.

Once back in my cell, I notice a piece of mail on my bunk. I flipped it over, and after seeing the return address, my heart sank. It was from the last person I expected to hear from—Ms. Karma Jolley. Steve was right. Her return address was at the Delta Charter Mental Health Center in Jackson, Mississippi. The envelope felt light, so I knew she hadn't written me some long, drawn out letter. I opened it and discovered a picture of the very pregnant Karma I didn't want to see. The back of it was a handwritten message, declaring for me not to worry because she was working on a plan that would put us back together soon. It was signed FOREVER YOURS, MRS. KARMA WEISMAN. Just as I was about to slide the photo back into the envelope, I noticed another picture was in there. I pulled it out.

"What the—," I yelled aloud.

Somehow, Karma had managed to obtain a photo of Aisha and Steve kissing as they sat on a bench in a park. His hand was on her breast, and her arms were wrapped around his neck. I turned the picture over and discovered the print date was about three months ago—shortly after I went into the slammer. I ran to the door of my cell then began beating on it.

BOOM, BOOM, BOOM

"Guard," I yelled. "Let me out! I need to make a phone call!"

BOOM, BOOM, BOOM

"Hey, anybody out there! I need to make a phone call! Let me out!"

I needed to get this new information over to my attorney. It seemed that the man I thought was my good friend had been burying me all along. I knew he was bored with Barbara, the holy-roller, and could possibly someday leave her for someone else, but I never thought he'd set sights on *my* wife.

What else did Karma know about Steve and this setup? Who would've thought: The woman I had declared my nemesis would now become my ally? I needed to speak with my attorney and quick! But, no one seemed to hear me except the other prisoners who yelled for me to shut up, or perhaps all of the deputies chose to ignore me. Either way, I was determined not to get tired, but the more I yelled, the more my voice began to fade in my own ears. Even still, someone would hear me today.

BOOM, BOOM, BOOM

"Guard! Heeeeyyyy! Let me out!"

Discussion Questions

1. What do you think of Lawrence (Doc) Weisman? Did you ever feel sorry for him? Why or why not?

2. How did you feel about Aisha? Did your feelings about her ever change? Why or why not?

3. Before having read the epilogue, how did you feel about Steven? Did you feel he was a true friend? Why or why not?

4. Did you sympathize with Darla? How did she go wrong?

5. Which of Karma's actions were extreme?

6. Should Audrie be mad at Cole for agreeing to participate in Lawrence's scheme? Why or why not?

7. Did WhiteKnight's identity surprise you? Talk about any other surprising elements of the story?

8. How realistic is the story of Karma and her psychiatrist? Do you feel there are real-life situations like theirs?

9. Did you ever sympathize with Karma? If so, when?

10. Based on the epilogue, can you determine how the rest of Karma's story would go? Please elaborate.

Acknowledgements

To God, I give all the Glory!

Much love to my daughters, Ebony and Imani. I'm so very proud of you both. I couldn't ask for better daughters!

Thank you to my loving and supporting parents, Charles and Rhonda Brown, Donald and Bobbie Smith, and much love to my siblings, Gregory, Ronald, Donna, and Bryant for your love and continued support.

To my precious grandma, Lillie Mae, I love you, but you cannot read this book. It is off limits. You can only read these acknowledgements. I know we've already had this discussion with my previous books, and I thank you for understanding. I love you, Grandma! ☺

To Uncle Paul (P.A. Tutwiler)—your turn! Write that book! To Uncle Ben (Benjamin Tutwiler)—how you like Karma now? Thank you both for always loving and supporting my work.

Much love and thanks to my sweetheart, Michael Finley, for always having my back. Words cannot express how much I love you.

To my best friend, Kendal Hubbard, much love to you, sis. We've had twenty-nine years of great friendship, and I count it a true blessing! Thanks for putting up with me and my books.

Mary Flucker and Mattie Ward, YOU ROCK!

To all those who love and support my work—thank you! I truly appreciate everyone who has been a part of my success and my literary endeavors.

About the Author

Playwright, Screenwriter, and National Bestselling Author, Alisha Yvonne is a native Memphian. She is the Essence® Bestselling Author of *Lovin' You Is Wrong* and *I Don't Wanna Be Right*. She is also nationally known for *Naughty Girls, The CleanUp Woman, Who's Fooling Who* and for having contributed to the bestseller, *Around the Way Girls-3*.

Alisha has taken her prolific skills to many levels as she has ventured into the nonfiction and young adult arenas. Look for her *Hopeland High* novels, *If I Were A Boy, Soulja Girl,* and the upcoming title, *Angel Among Us*. She is currently working on her next adult fiction book.

Visit Alisha online at www.alishayvonne.com or email to: alisha@ebonyliterarygrace.com

www.ingramcontent.com/pod-product-compliance
Lightning Source LLC
Chambersburg PA
CBHW070322260626
47160CB00003B/924